"You need to stay inside, Colton. And keep away from the windows," Jasmine whispered.

He bristled. He was probably used to being the protector. "You're supposed to stay with Liam."

"No, I'm supposed to protect Liam and, in the process, also protect you. Right now, there may be a threat out there. I'd suggest you let me go investigate."

Jaw still tight, Colton dropped his hand and gave Jasmine a sharp nod.

She drew her weapon and opened the door enough to slip through. "Lock this behind me. Don't open it unless I give you an all clear."

Colton's dog Brutus was on the right side of the house, still barking. When Jasmine rounded the corner, Brutus stood with his back to her, facing the front yard. He'd stopped barking, but deep growls rumbled in his chest, and his body rippled with tension.

A rustle sounded a few yards to the side of them, raising the fine hairs on the back of Jasmine's neck. Every sense shot to full alert with the impending threat of an ambush...

Carol J. Post writes fun and fast-paced inspirational romantic suspense stories and lives in sunshiny central Florida. She sings and plays the piano for her church and also enjoys sailing, hiking and camping—almost anything outdoors. Her daughters and grandkids live too far away for her liking, so she now pours all that nurturing into taking care of two fat and sassy cats and one highly spoiled dachshund.

Books by Carol J. Post

Love Inspired Suspense

BODYGUARD FOR CHRISTMAS

CAROL J. POST

HARLEQUIN® LOVE INSPIRED® SUSPENSE

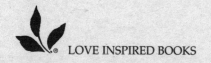 LOVE INSPIRED BOOKS

Recycling programs
for this product may
not exist in your area.

ISBN-13: 978-1-335-49079-7

Bodyguard for Christmas

Copyright © 2018 by Carol J. Post

He healeth the broken in heart,
and bindeth up their wounds.
–Psalms 147:3

Thank you to all the people who supported me
in writing this series:

My sister Kim, for all the help with research,
My critique partners Karen Fleming and Sabrina Jarema,
Mom Post for beta/proofreading,
My editor Dina Davis and my agent, Nalini Akolekar,
My sweet, supportive family,
And my loving husband, Chris.

ONE

The wrought iron gate swung inward under a steel-gray sky. Colton Gale eased his Highlander through the opening to climb the road leading into his Atlanta subdivision.

Passing between those large brick columns used to always bring a sense of contentment and warmth. Maybe someday he'd find it again.

"You all right, bro?"

Colton glanced at his twin in the front passenger seat. For someone who lived life flying by the seat of his pants, Cade could be remarkably perceptive.

Colton forced a half smile. "Yeah."

Cade nodded, silent assent to let it drop rather than acceptance or agreement. "Thanks for going with me this morning. Since you've been back in town only a week, I know you've got other things to do."

"No problem."

When their father retired, he'd signed over the antiquities business to both of them. As co-owner, Colton's signature was required for official business, like renewing their line of credit, which they'd done that morning.

But giving his John Hancock when needed was where his involvement ended. His job as an assistant district attorney kept him plenty busy. Besides, Cade was the one with the art and antiquities degree. He was also an expert schmoozer. Everyone seemed to let down their guard and trust him, whether it was warranted or not.

Colton rounded a gentle curve, where a huge oak spread half-bare limbs over the road, then cast another glance at his brother. Though their looks were identical, he'd never had Cade's charisma.

Now the differences in their personalities were even more pronounced. For Colton, studious and sincere had become almost brooding. Though Cade had tried to pull him into the social scene, Colton wasn't interested. The transition from widowed to single and available didn't happen overnight. Even six months later, putting on a party face required more effort than he was willing to give.

He heaved a sigh. He knew the platitudes. He'd used them himself—*Life is short. No one is guaranteed tomorrow.* Somehow, he'd thought those were for other people. The last thing he'd expected was for tragedy to strike his own perfectly ordered life.

"When we get to your house, I'll have to leave to get to my appointment." Cade's words cut across his thoughts.

Colton nodded. He'd expected as much. The business at the company's bank had taken longer than anticipated. Little Liam would be disappointed. He adored his uncle Cade. Anytime Cade stopped by, Liam always tried to talk him into staying longer.

Well, *talk* was a misnomer. Except for during frequent nightmares, Colton's son hadn't said a word in almost six months. But the silent pleas with those big brown eyes were just about as effective.

Colton rounded a gentle right curve. These were his favorite homesites, with yards that backed up to the stucco wall that surrounded the subdivision, woods beyond.

"Stop." Cade held up a hand. "Pull over."

He hit the brake, following his brother's gaze out the passenger window. A pickup truck was parked in the circle drive in front of the house catty-corner from his. A woman slid a five-gallon bucket from the bed onto the tailgate.

The place had been for sale when he'd left town. Someone had apparently bought it and was doing renovations. From what he'd heard, it had needed it.

Cade put his hand on the door handle. "Have you met your new neighbor? She's pretty hot when she's not covered in drywall dust."

"I thought you had an appointment."

"I do. But I can always make time for a lady, especially when it involves introducing one to my stick-in-the-mud brother."

Great. When Colton's life had fallen apart and he'd needed to get away, Cade had been at the end of his apartment lease and happy to house-sit. During his almost five months here, he'd probably checked out every single woman in the neighborhood. "I don't need to be introduced."

"We can at least be gentlemen and help her unload those buckets of paint."

Colton heaved a sigh, killing the engine, then followed his brother up the drive. The woman cast them a glance, then did a double take. "Whoa, you guys must be twins. One of you is Cade."

Cade raised a hand. "That would be me. And this is Colton, the smarter, better-looking one."

Her mouth split into a wide smile, and her dark eyes sparkled below a pixie haircut a shade deeper. He could see why Cade would classify her as "hot."

Cade had a variety of preferences. Colton measured

every woman against one. The comparisons weren't intentional. They just happened, like a deeply ingrained habit. The thoughts were pointless, because he wasn't even considering dating, regardless of his meddling brother's efforts.

The woman extended her hand. "Jasmine McNeal. I'm hoping to have this place move-in ready in another two weeks." After a firm handshake, she turned back to the truck and reached for the paint bucket.

Colton stepped forward. "Let us get those for you."

"I can handle them."

Yeah, she probably could. She was short, didn't even reach his shoulders. Jeans and a sweatshirt hid her build, but judging from the way she was handling the paint bucket, she was probably well acquainted with the gym.

But he wasn't the type to watch a woman haul construction supplies, no matter how strong she seemed. While she lowered one bucket to the concrete driveway, he reached into the bed and pulled out the second one.

Cade closed the tailgate. "Sorry to greet and run, but I've got an appointment." He started down the driveway at a half jog, throwing the next words over his shoulder. "I'm borrowing your gate control. I'll put it back in your car before I leave."

Colton followed his new neighbor into the house and placed the second bucket on the concrete floor next to hers. Everywhere he could see, carpet had been removed. The walls had numerous patches varying from fist-size to more than a foot in diameter.

She followed his gaze. "Pretty bad, huh? The old owners were carrying the mortgage, and when they had to foreclose, the new people got ticked and totally trashed the place. I'm making progress, though. Someone's bringing in a hopper tomorrow and texturing the walls. Then I'll be ready to paint."

She leaned against the doorjamb between the living and dining rooms. "So, are you visiting Cade?"

"The other way around. Cade was house-sitting for me while I've been gone. He's pretty well moved out now."

Over the past week, while Cade had worked on gathering his possessions, Colton had done some clearing out of his own, a task that had hung over him for the past half a year. The first four weeks, he hadn't been able to even think about it. He still wasn't ready, but it was time.

So three boxes occupied his back seat, with several more packed into the rear. He'd planned to drop the clothing by a thrift store and put the jewelry in the safety deposit box at his own bank. He hadn't made it to either place before having to get Cade back home. He'd have to run back out this afternoon.

She walked with him to the door. "Thanks for toting the paint."

"No problem." When he stepped outside, a single beam of late November sunshine had found its way through the clouds blanketing the sky. Across the street, Cade was backing his Corvette through the wrought iron gate at the end of Colton's driveway. What stood a short distance beyond wasn't the most extravagant residence in the neighborhood, but the yard was neatly manicured and the three-bedroom, two-bath home exuded warmth and elegance. Not bad for a former foster kid.

The gate rolled closed, and Cade stopped next to Colton's Highlander to return the control. Although the community was gated, the wrought iron fence that circled his property added an extra layer of protection. So did the rottweiler who regularly circled the half-acre grounds surrounding his home.

Except Brutus wasn't waiting at the fence. A vague sense of unease wove through him as he scanned the yard. In his job as an assistant district attorney, he'd made some enemies and received several threats. Most he hadn't taken seriously. A few he had.

He wished his new neighbor farewell and hurried to his vehicle. At a push of a button, the gate rolled open. Still no dog. The uneasiness intensified.

Colton slid from the Highlander and hurried toward the house. Nothing looked amiss in front.

But where was his dog?

He climbed the porch steps, heart pounding. His three-year-old son and babysitter were inside. He fumbled as he tried to insert the key into the lock. When he finally swung open the door, fear morphed to panic. At the opposite end of the foyer, every drawer in the Bombay chest was open, the contents strewn across the top and overflowing onto the tile floor. On either side, the living room and den were in the same condition.

"Liam!" He ran into the family room. "Meagan!" Where were they?

Dear God, let them be okay.

He headed toward the hall. At half past one, Meagan would have already put Liam down for his nap.

Movement snapped his gaze toward the dining room. As Colton ran into the room, a figure disappeared through the back door, little legs bouncing on either side of his waist. Colton's knees went weak, almost buckling under him.

Someone was taking his son.

He tore into the room, shattered glass on the floor barely registering before he burst through the back door. Two figures ran toward the rear fence, knit ski masks covering their heads. At his shout, the man carrying Liam turned, then dropped his burden.

Liam hit the ground and landed in a heap, legs curled under him, face turned to the side. A vise clamped down on Colton's chest. Liam wasn't moving. *Oh, God, please…*

No, if the men had harmed him, they wouldn't be trying to kidnap him.

When he dropped to his knees next to his son, his breath whooshed out. Liam was breathing. His eyes were squeezed shut, and soft whimpers slipped through his parted lips. Colton scooped him up, and little arms went around his neck with a strength that surprised him.

Rapid footsteps approached, and Colton swiveled his head. "Meag—"

But it wasn't Meagan who'd stopped a short distance away, face etched with concern. It was his new neighbor. What was she doing there?

He rose, clutching Liam to his chest. "I have to find my babysitter."

Jasmine shifted her attention to the back of his property, and he followed her gaze. A man dropped from one of the lower limbs of his oak tree to disappear behind the wall. A second shimmied out to follow his accomplice.

Colton squeezed his son more tightly. He'd get a tree trimmer out pronto. That same branch had probably given them a way into the property.

As he turned, a dark shape snagged his gaze. It lay several yards from the oak's trunk, partially obscured by the shrubbery lining the back wall. Brutus. He pressed his lips together. As soon as he found Meagan, he'd check on his dog.

When he looked at Jasmine again, she was already punching numbers into her phone. "I'm calling 911."

"Thanks." He'd let her handle it. He ran back to the house. Next to the door, jagged glass surrounded a large hole in the dining room window. He'd check out the security footage later. Or the cops would. He had a camera in back and one in front.

Once inside, he ran room to room, still holding his son while he shouted Meagan's name. An image rose in his mind—features twisted, hatred shining from eyes so dark they were almost black. One defendant whose threats had sent a chill all the way to his core.

Colton had gotten the man a life sentence. Death would have been better. Drug dealer, gang leader and ruthless killer—men like that didn't rehabilitate. Before being led from the courtroom in shackles, he'd turned to Colton and made his threat, cold fury flowing beneath the surface. *You didn't get a death sentence for me, but you just secured your own.*

Maybe Perez *had* sent someone for him, and taking Liam was his way of drawing Colton out. Or maybe it was someone else, determined to exact the worst kind of vengeance.

When he started down the hall, a cell phone lay on the floor. Meagan's phone. His chest clenched. Eighteen years old, her whole life ahead of her.

Oh, God, please let her be safe.

As he stepped into his son's room, Liam stiffened and let out a wail. Colton cupped the back of his head. "It's okay, buddy."

He looked around the room. Drawers hung open, their contents tossed to the floor. Nearby, a Lego village sat in a state of incompletion. Maybe this was where Liam had been playing when the man grabbed him.

Jasmine stepped up behind him. "Cops are on the way.

I checked on your dog. He's unconscious, but his breathing is steady. What happened?"

"Someone just tried to kidnap my son. My house is ransacked and my babysitter's missing." He spun to walk from the room.

She stepped out of his way. "Maybe she escaped when the men broke in."

"And left Liam inside? Not Meagan."

"Or she could have slipped out to call the police."

He walked into the bathroom across the hall. "They'd have been here long before now." The destruction they were looking at didn't happen in minutes. "She's here somewhere. She'd never abandon Liam to save—"

Colton cut off his own thought. Had he just heard a thud? His gaze snapped to his neighbor. She'd obviously heard it, too.

He jogged down the hall toward the master bedroom. When he called Meagan's name again, the thuds grew louder, more insistent. As he entered the room, there was another thud, and the door on the large walk-in closet jumped. He shifted Liam to one hip and swung it back on the hinges.

Meagan lay curled on the floor, hands tied behind her back, ankles bound. Tape covered her mouth. An angry bruise was already forming on her left cheek. When her fear-filled eyes met his, they welled with tears.

Colton tried to pry his son loose, but Liam released a wail that built into a scream of pure terror.

"Here, let me." Jasmine pushed Colton aside and dropped to her knees. "This is going to hurt."

When she ripped the tape from the girl's face, Meagan winced. "I tried to protect him." The tears flowed in earnest now.

"He's fine." Jasmine looked at Colton. "Get me something to cut the rope."

He pulled a pocketknife from the drawer in his bedside stand. Jasmine had stepped in and taken charge. With a terrified child and a babysitter on the verge of hysteria, he was thankful for the help.

"Why did you come?"

"You." Without looking up, she continued sawing through the ropes binding Meagan's ankles. "When Cade was leaving, you started acting weird, like you were worried about something. I figured I'd stay outside and watch you."

Colton shook his head. He'd just met the woman. How could she identify *weird* when she had nothing to base *normal* on? Had to be women's intuition. After seven years of marriage, he still didn't understand it.

"When you left your front door wide-open, I knew something was up." The last rope gave way. Jasmine helped a sobbing Meagan to her feet and led her to the bed. "It's okay. You're safe now."

Colton sat next to his babysitter, Liam in his lap. "What happened?"

"Liam and I were sitting on the floor playing with his Legos when I heard glass shatter." She drew in a shuddering breath, struggling to pull herself together. "I jumped up to get my phone. I'd left it on the coffee table in the living room."

She swiped at her tears. "I got halfway back to the bedroom when someone tackled me from behind. He was straddling me, flipped me over and punched me in the head. Everything went black. I just woke up a few minutes ago."

She squeezed her eyes shut. Today's events would likely trigger some terrifying nightmares.

He put a hand on her shoulder. "Do you know who attacked you?"

"He was wearing a ski mask." The tears started anew. "All I could think about was Liam." She stroked his back. "Is he all right?"

"Just frightened."

Colton had no idea what his son had witnessed and probably wouldn't anytime soon. Liam had stopped speaking shortly after his mother died.

"Uh, Colton?"

Something in Jasmine's tone sent fingers of dread crawling down his spine. He followed her gaze toward the door.

His mahogany dresser occupied a sizable section of the wall to the right of it, the massive mirror framed by curved shelves on either side. Letters were scrawled across the glass in his dead wife's lipstick.

His foundation shifted, and the room seemed to tilt sideways as the message dived deep into his heart.

"The sins of the fathers…"

From the time he was adopted at age fifteen, he'd attended church. He knew his Bible. The next words went something like "…are visited on the children to the third and fourth generation." Whoever wrote the phrase was taking the verse out of context, but the intended meaning was clear.

Colton tightened his hold on Liam and buried his face in the boy's hair, soft and silky like his mother's had been. Determination surged through him. No one was going to get to his son ever again. He'd see to it.

Sirens wailed outside, growing in volume. Soon the police would be there. He'd give his report. And he'd insist that Meagan go to the hospital.

Then he'd find a bodyguard. Someone big and tough and mean.

The fence encircling the yard, with its electronic gate, the rottweiler prowling the property, the alarm when they were asleep. It wasn't enough. What had previously been empty threats had just taken on flesh and blood.

He'd do whatever he must to ensure Liam's safety. Even if it meant paying for around-the-clock protection.

Or leaving Atlanta and starting over somewhere else. Maybe both.

Yes, definitely both.

Jasmine strode down the hall of Burch Security Specialists, her gait heavier than normal. She still had another week blocked off, which would have given her enough time to finish the interior painting before the scheduled carpet installation began. So much for plans. Less than an hour ago, she'd gotten a call from her boss and former commander—she needed to show up pronto for a new assignment.

Gunn didn't tell her what the assignment was, but something in his tone warned her. She was about to meet another idiot who had his doubts about whether a woman could handle the job. After doing two tours with her in Afghanistan, Gunn didn't have any of those reservations.

She stopped at the end of the hall. A plaque was affixed next to a closed door—*Gunter Burch, Owner* in engraved black letters. At her two soft raps, Gunn's voice boomed a command to enter.

A man sat facing Gunn's desk, his back to her. He was wearing a suit, sandy-blond hair brushing the jacket's collar.

"Colton Gale, Jasmine McNeal." Gunn indicated her with a tilt of his head.

Her jaw slackened when Gunn gave the visitor's name. "We've met." They spoke the words simultaneously.

"It's good to see you again." Colton stood and extended his hand, pinning her with his blue gaze.

Yesterday, his eyes had held panic, desperation, protectiveness. Now a sadness she hadn't noticed swam in their depths. When he smiled, there was a tightness to it, as if it had been so long since he'd given the gesture a try it no longer came naturally. He and Cade were identical twins, but they wore their personality differences on their faces.

Jasmine accepted the handshake, her grip firm and confident. Colton probably had her five feet two inches beat by a solid foot. The one-inch heel on her boots didn't make any appreciable difference. He still towered over her.

He wasn't in bad shape, either, especially for a business type. His jacket hung open. Beneath the dress shirt and narrow tie, the guy was obviously fit. Of course, she'd suspected that yesterday, too.

Colton released her hand. "I take it you work here?"

"For the past three years." They hadn't exchanged personal details yesterday. He'd helped her carry in a bucket of paint, then left. At his place, they'd been occupied with more important things.

"What do you do for the company?"

Great. He probably thought she did clerical work. Gunn did that on purpose—referred to her by her nickname when talking to potentially difficult clients and introduced her by her legal name in person.

She straightened the zippered black jacket she wore and lifted her chin. "Bodyguard. Former MP."

He cocked a brow for a half second before understanding flooded his eyes. "Jaz. Jasmine." His jaw tightened, and his gaze went to Gunn. "This isn't what I had in mind."

Jasmine bristled. "I'm sure he told you my qualifications."

Those blue eyes turned to her again. But the sadness she'd seen was buried under layers of determination. "He did. But I'd assumed Jaz was a man."

Heat built in her chest and spread. "You felt those qualifications were impressive until you found out they belonged to a woman."

"I know this sounds sexist. I don't mean it that way." He heaved a sigh. "You know what I came home to yesterday. No offense, but I'm looking for someone a little more…intimidating."

Yeah, someone like her coworker Dom. But Gunn knew what he was doing. Other than the fact that the former sniper was assigned elsewhere, he was built like a linebacker and unintentionally terrified small children.

She drew in a calming breath. Colton was trying to protect his little boy. The reminder was like water splashed on a fire. Enough to slow it down but a long way from dousing it completely.

He continued before she had a chance to respond. "I'm an assistant district attorney, and I've put away some really bad dudes. One has decided to go after my son." He crossed his arms. "I'm sure you're good at what you do, but I need somebody big and mean."

He stared down at her, exuding an unmistakable sense of power. In the courtroom, he was probably a force to be reckoned with.

But when it came to protection, so was she. "A thirty-eight stops a man cold, regardless of the size of the hand holding it."

"What if someone sneaks up behind you?"

"They'd better hit me with a tranquilizer dart first."

"That's exactly what they did to my dog."

Oh. "You're assuming they could get close enough. Not gonna happen."

He dropped his arms to his sides. His gaze swept downward to her feet and back up again. Something changed. His eyes held a momentary flash of indecision, then coldness.

She stepped back with her right foot, weight distributed equally between both legs, knees slightly bent. She didn't get where she was by not being able to read people. Unless she'd completely lost her touch, Colton Gale was preparing to administer a test.

One she was determined to pass.

He lunged toward her, arms swinging upward to capture her. She didn't give him the opportunity to complete the maneuver. In one smooth motion, she grasped his arm, twisted, crouched and thrust one hip into his legs. Using his own weight and momentum against him, she jerked him forward as she straightened.

He sailed over her, did a flip and landed hard on his back, the plush carpet muffling the thud. Before he could recover, she rolled him over, dropped to one knee and wrenched his right arm behind his back.

He slapped the floor like a wrestler conceding a match. "Okay." His voice sounded strained. "Point taken."

She held him a moment longer before releasing him, then rose and watched him get to his feet. "So, tell me about my assignment." The words were for Gunn, but she kept her gaze locked on her tall neighbor.

"You're going to live at their home. While Mr. Gale is there, you'll be responsible for protecting both of them."

Colton settled himself in the chair where he'd been

when she first entered. "But Liam will be your first responsibility."

"Understood."

She tamped down her annoyance and sank into the chair next to him. Dom likely never had potential clients doubt his competence. The other three Burch Security people probably didn't, either. Though not as large as Dom, they were all men.

Colton continued. "Tomorrow morning, we're heading to Murphy, North Carolina, two hours north. We moved from there a year ago." He heaved a tension-filled sigh. "Probably should have never left."

The last words were soft, like a private thought that spilled out without him realizing it. Life had apparently not gone the way he'd hoped. Of course, that was typical for those who walked through Burch Security's door. People didn't need a bodyguard when everything was sunshine and roses.

"Where is Liam now?"

"With Cade."

Colton's brother rather than his wife. Maybe he was a single parent.

She frowned. She wasn't good with kids, particularly ones that young. At least, that was what she assumed. In actuality, she'd managed to avoid them. With the exception of a sixteen-year-old amateur model who'd picked up a stalker, all her assignments had involved adults.

"When do I start?"

"Tonight." Gunn tapped a pen on his desk. "I'll fill you in on what you need to know. Then you can get your personal belongings together. Corine will be in touch with you after she checks out the leads Mr. Gale gave us."

She nodded. Corine had worked for Burch Security since a month after Gunn opened shop, and she was a whiz on the computer. If there was information available, she'd find it.

Colton continued. "By nine tomorrow morning, I want to be on my way to Murphy. The sooner we leave Atlanta, the better I'll feel. Whoever's threatening us likely doesn't know about the Murphy house."

A good reason to go there. But likely not Colton's only reason. Whenever he spoke of Murphy, his tone held a solid dose of nostalgia. It wasn't just a physical haven. It was likely an emotional one, too.

But beyond providing a safe place to stay, relocating wouldn't fix anything. Whatever had transpired over the past year, Colton couldn't make it *un*happen. Time went forward, never backward. Water that flowed under the bridge never came back.

How well she knew.

"Then I guess it's settled." He pushed himself to his feet. "You know where I live. See you in two hours?"

"Two hours." She stood and extended her hand.

After finishing the handshake, he reached across his torso to massage his right arm. One side of his mouth lifted almost imperceptibly. "Do you always rough up your new clients?"

"Only the ones who need it."

The smile broadened just a tad. "Staying in Murphy should make your job a lot easier." That thread of a smile disappeared completely. "As long as we're not followed."

She gave a sharp nod. "It'll be my responsibility to make sure we're not."

TWO

The security system's high-pitched beep punctuated the thunk of the dead bolt as Colton locked the front door. He had no idea when he'd return. After one week back on the job following an almost five-month leave of absence, he'd resigned his position with the district attorney's office.

Cade had come back after his appointment Thursday afternoon and done a thorough search of the house, making sure he'd moved the last of his possessions. The break-in had shaken him. Apparently, it had taken almost losing his nephew to make him realize life wasn't just one cosmic joke.

Colton turned from the door, Liam perched on his hip. This time, the house would sit empty. Not only had Cade gotten an apartment, he wasn't even going to be in town for the next month. He'd teased that he didn't want to be mistaken for Colton.

In reality, he'd gotten leads on some collections to be auctioned off. Cade's plans often changed at the last moment. The lifestyle suited him well. He didn't let anything tie him down, which was why he'd never bought a house, even though he could afford it. Home ownership felt too much like commitment.

Colton headed down the porch steps. A black Subur-

ban waited behind his Highlander. Jasmine stood next
to the driver's door.

Her eyes shifted to him briefly before she went back
to scanning their surroundings, ever vigilant. She'd spent
the night and slept on the daybed in Liam's room. Thursday night, Liam had awoken screaming so many times
Colton had lost count. Last night's sleep had been bliss-
fully free of nightmares, at least for his son. Unfortunately, he'd had a few of his own.

As Colton swung open his rear driver door, Jasmine
continued to stand guard. Her presence brought just the
sense of security he'd hoped.

Before leaving Burch Security yesterday, he'd signed
the necessary paperwork. As he had written the check
for the first payment, Gunter Burch had reassured him
of Jasmine's qualifications. Between her military background, her civilian assignments and all the advanced
training in both capacities, he and Liam were going to
be in good hands. Of course, eating carpet fibers had already dispelled whatever doubts he'd had.

Jasmine's eyes shifted to him, and he nodded. Yes, he
was ready. More than ready.

She opened the Suburban's door. "I'll be behind you,
but I might hang back on the interstate. Keep your phone
plugged into your car's stereo system. Anything suspicious, I'll let you know."

"Thank you." She was only doing her job, a job that
was costing him a pretty penny. But that didn't stop him
from appreciating everything she was doing to protect
them.

He leaned into the vehicle to secure Liam in his car
seat. Brutus sat next to him, tail thumping against leather.
Huge brown eyes seemed to hold sadness, maybe even
guilt, as if the dog sensed he'd failed in his job to protect.

Colton fastened the last latch, then leaned across Liam to pet Brutus. "It's okay, buddy. It wasn't your fault."

He straightened and closed the door. Yesterday morning, before going to Burch Security, he'd taken care of the things he hadn't gotten to on Thursday. Mandy's jewelry was now locked in his safety deposit box.

Then he'd gone to a thrift store and parked at the open bay door in back. It had taken all the strength he had to climb from the vehicle and pull out the first box. With each one he passed to the volunteer, he'd felt as if he was handing over a piece of his heart.

Now it was done, and several suitcases holding his and Liam's possessions occupied the space behind the back seat. He'd packed everything he could think of. Anything he'd forgotten, he'd buy in Murphy.

The investigation was far from complete. Cops had viewed the security footage. Besides the knit masks, the intruders had worn gloves, so the likelihood of recovering prints was nil.

As he drove through the subdivision's exit gate, some of the tension flowed out of him. In two more hours, he'd be pulling up the drive and stopping in front of the log home with its soaring windows and steeply pitched roof.

Warm, cozy and filled with love, it had always held a special place in his heart. He and Mandy had purchased it six years earlier for a weekend getaway and built so many memories.

Four years ago, he and his pregnant wife had decided Murphy was a perfect place to raise children, and they'd made the move. Until the district attorney's office had lured him back.

Now he was going home.

After several turns, he accelerated up the I-285 ramp. The black Suburban was right behind him, Jasmine at the wheel. Dark sunglasses shielded her eyes. But he didn't need to see them to know she was watching traffic in more than a defensive-driving sense.

He craned his neck to glance at his son in the rearview mirror. As expected, he was awake, left arm clutching his plush rabbit, right thumb in his mouth. Another change Colton had noticed. As Liam's speech had gotten less, soon stopping completely, his thumb sucking had gone from only when sleeping to almost all the time. Colton would have to address it eventually, but certainly not now.

He moved into the left lane and accelerated. Varying his speed would make it harder for someone to follow him, at least without Jasmine noticing. He checked his mirrors. On a Saturday morning, traffic was moderate. The Suburban was some distance back, traveling in the right lane. He signaled and prepared to merge onto I-75. As he decreased his speed, several vehicles went around him. He moved into the far-right lane and exited 285 in front of a slow-moving dump truck.

After several miles, he picked up speed again. Soon he'd be on 575, headed toward Murphy. An unexpected sense of anticipation wove through him.

He'd made this move twice before. Each time, it had represented a fresh start, and he'd found freedom, happiness, a sense of belonging.

The first time, he'd been fifteen, leaving behind years in foster care to become part of a real family. The second time, he'd been filled with excitement, ready to start his own family.

This would be a new start also, one he'd never hoped to make. He and Liam, facing an uncertain future, their family unit shattered. Hoping to stay hidden from someone who might want them dead.

The phone's ringtone cut across his thoughts. It was Jasmine.

"Don't take the 575 exit. I think you have a tail."

His pulse picked up speed, and an instant sheet of moisture coated his palms. "Which vehicle?"

"The silver Mustang."

He looked in his rearview mirror. There it was, one lane to his left, about five cars back. "Can you slow down, get a tag number?"

"I've tried. I think he knows I'm with you. Whenever I drop back, he does, too. Won't give me an opportunity to read his tag."

"What do you have in mind?"

"Ernest Barrett Parkway is the next exit. Easy off, easy on."

After he disconnected the call, Jasmine slowed down so much he almost lost sight of her. Several cars moved between them. The Mustang didn't.

As he approached 575, the GPS told him to exit. He ignored it. Jasmine was in charge and he had no problem letting her call the shots.

After he exited I-75, the light ahead was red. He eased to a stop, then dialed her back. "Did our friend follow?"

"I'm not sure, but I think he's behind the box truck."

He counted the vehicles lined up in his rearview mirror. In their lane, three waited between him and Jasmine, two more between her and the box truck. Likely every one of them would turn left on Ernest Barrett. If the Mustang followed him and Jasmine back onto 75, they'd know for sure.

The light changed, and he moved forward. As he made his way up the on-ramp, two vehicles followed from Ernest Barrett, a semitruck blocking any farther view.

He completed his merge and touched the phone, still

clipped into the dash mount. Jasmine's rang four times, then went to voice mail.

Maybe she was calling the police, which meant someone was following them. A sense of protectiveness gripped him, an urge to wrap Liam in his arms so tightly no one could pry him loose.

Colton lifted his chin until the rearview mirror framed his son's face. Sad eyes looked back at him. Brown, just like his mother's. Liam had gotten Mandy's eyes and Colton's blond hair.

When his phone rang a few minutes later, he swiped the screen, heart racing while he waited for Jasmine's update.

"Sorry, I was on the phone with 911 when you called. He followed us back onto the interstate, hanging back like before. But he knew we were onto him. He got off on Chastain Road, no signal, just whipped it over. The police know to look for the car there, but I'm not holding out high hopes."

He wasn't, either. "What now? Exit, then head back south to pick up 575?"

"Not knowing where that Mustang is, I say we continue north and take 411 near Cartersville. It might be a little out of the way, but it's better than running across those guys again."

The next two hours were uneventful. When he finally pulled onto Hilltop Road, several miles southwest of town, all of nature seemed to wrap him in a comforting embrace. He was home. The quaintness, the low crime rate, the small-town atmosphere, the feeling of having stepped back into a safer, slower, less complicated time— Murphy was still a great place to raise a child.

He stayed left where the road forked and wound his way upward. He hadn't been back since Mandy died.

For weeks, he'd stumbled around in a grief-induced fog, somehow managing after a two-week bereavement leave to return to his duties and care for Liam when he wasn't working.

A week later, he'd gotten word that Mandy's father had had a heart attack. Though he'd survived, it was going to be a long road to recovery. Having just lost their only child, they'd had no one to turn to.

So Colton had taken a leave of absence, loaded up Liam and headed to Montana. He wasn't sure who had benefited the most from his trip out West. He'd gone to help his in-laws. But in those quiet moments, sitting on the back deck as the sun sank behind the mountains and daylight turned to dusk, then darkness, God had ministered to him. Little by little the frayed pieces of his heart had begun to heal.

Near the top of the hill, he pulled into a gravel drive. A huge hemlock rose from the center of the front yard, hiding the majority of the A-frame log cabin from the view of the road. Trees huddled around the other three sides of the house. The hardwoods' limbs were bare except for the most stubborn leaves. Brown and curled, they were determined to hang on until they had no choice but to succumb to winter's fury.

Colton put the vehicle in Park and turned in his seat. "We're here, buddy. Our favorite place."

The excitement he tried to inject into his tone had no effect on Liam. He didn't expect it to. Every week, his little boy seemed to retreat a bit more into himself. And Colton had no idea how to help him. Apparently, his counselors hadn't, either, because nothing had seemed to work.

Colton climbed from the vehicle and removed his son from the car seat. After retrieving one of the suitcases, he walked up the sidewalk, Liam's hand in his. Halfway there, Liam broke away and ran toward the house. When he reached the front deck, he looked over one shoulder. Hope had replaced the vacancy in his eyes.

Colton's heart swelled with emotion. Liam remembered the place.

Of course he did. It was where he'd lived the first year and a half of his life and where they'd spent almost every weekend after that until the past six months.

As soon as Colton opened the door, Liam burst through. He crossed the living room at a full run, skidded around the bar that marked the boundary of the kitchen and disappeared into the bedroom to the right. Colton smiled, laughter bubbling up inside. It was the first glimpse he'd seen of the carefree little boy he used to have. Coming back to Murphy was the best thing he could have done for his son.

Liam reappeared moments later. After running into the master bedroom, he returned to the living room. His gait was shuffling, every bit of excitement gone. Had he worn himself out that quickly?

Colton dropped to one knee in front of him. "What's the matter, buddy?"

Liam's lower lip quivered, and his eyes filled with tears.

Colton sank the rest of the way to the floor, realization kicking him hard in the chest.

Liam wasn't happy to be back in Murphy.

He was looking for his mother.

Colton stretched out his arms and grasped his son's hands. "Sweetheart, Mommy's not here."

When he'd pulled him onto his lap, he wrapped his arms around his little body and held him tightly, rocking side to side, seeking to comfort himself as much as his son.

Movement drew his attention to the left. Jasmine stood in the open doorway, her purse hanging from her shoulder and a suitcase in each hand. She didn't say a word, but the sympathy in her gaze spoke volumes. She'd had her own heartaches.

Maybe having her there would help ease some of Liam's sorrow and loneliness. Maybe it would help ease some of his own.

No, Jasmine wasn't a mother figure. And she certainly wasn't a wife. That wasn't why he'd hired her. He'd hired her to protect him and his son.

Once the assignment was over, she'd be gone.

No one would ever take Mandy's place.

Not in his life or his son's.

Jasmine parted the curtains and peered into the front yard. Late afternoon shadows stretched across the landscape. Security here was minimal. Actually, it was nonexistent, something that would be remedied this week.

Shortly after arriving at the Murphy house three days ago, she'd walked the premises and come up with a security plan. An alarm system was a minimum requirement. Before the weekend, all windows and doors would be wired and motion-sensing lights installed on the perimeter of the house. For the time being, camera installation was on hold. But it would be scheduled immediately if she felt the need.

She let the cloth panel drop. For the past thirty minutes, she'd made her rounds to several of the house's windows, checking on Liam in between. This residence wasn't elegant like Colton's Atlanta home. But with hardwood floors, tongue-and-groove walls and a fireplace tucked into one side of the living room, it was nice—cozy and rustic. And as long as Colton's enemies didn't know he was here, it was safe.

Ideally, she'd have backup, a second or third bodyguard to help patrol and provide relief. But Colton didn't have as deep pockets as Burch's celebrity and big-business clients, especially after the extended leave of absence to care for his in-laws—one of the things she'd learned from Gunn after Colton had left the office Friday. If he'd remained in Atlanta, they wouldn't have given him a choice.

The ringtone sounded on her phone, and she released it from the clip on her belt. The screen ID'd Burch Security as the caller.

Corine's Southern twang came through the phone. "I've checked out some of the names Mr. Gale gave Gunn. I'm still working on it, but there are two people who match the description of the men who tried to kidnap his son. At least their size. Since they were wearing ski masks, that's all we've got to go on."

"Who?"

"Richard Perez is the first name Gale gave us. Turns out, he has regular visits from his brothers. Both have records, but they're out now. The older one is tall and lanky. The younger one is close to the same height but built like an offensive lineman."

Jasmine nodded. "It fits."

"Another name Gale gave us is Broderick 'Ace' Hoffman, who was released three weeks ago. He's roughly the same size as the thinner guy. We're checking out people he's known to associate with to see if any of them fit the other guy's description."

As Corine continued to provide information, Jasmine moved to the back door and peered through the paned glass inset. Finally, the admin fell silent.

"Anyone else?" Corine had given her six possible matches.

"That's it for now. You know Gale's wife died of natural causes, right?"

"Yeah, Gunn gave me all the history."

After ending the call, she glanced through the open doorway to Liam's room. Keeping track of the boy was the easy part of her assignment. He wasn't a typical preschooler, with boundless energy and a touch of mischievousness. Instead, he seemed perfectly content to play quietly on the floor.

He was also spending his days in preschool. Colton had enrolled him yesterday, after securing his former job with the district attorney's office for Cherokee County. He'd given her two reasons for the preschool decision. One, he hadn't hired her to be a babysitter. She couldn't agree more.

Two, he didn't want his son spending so much time with her that he'd get attached. More good thinking. Liam's mother was no longer in the picture, and he wasn't handling it well.

She'd abide by Colton's wishes and not let Liam get attached to her. But the sad little boy she'd been charged with protecting stirred something in her. Twenty-five years ago, that had been her—quiet, withdrawn, tormented by nightmares. Unlike Liam, she'd had a mother throughout most of her childhood. And her mother loved her. She'd just been too young and dysfunctional to know how to raise a child.

Jasmine leaned against Liam's doorjamb, and his eyes met hers. He sat amid a sea of Legos, an almost completed rectangular object in front of him.

She stepped into the room. "What are you building?"

He lowered his gaze and searched through the pieces

until he found a truss-shaped one, then snapped it onto an end.

"Are you building a house?"

Liam continued his project without making eye contact again. She turned to leave the room. She'd never been good at one-sided conversations.

At the door, she hesitated. A chest of drawers sat to its right, a framed eight-by-ten photograph on top. She'd noticed it there before but hadn't taken the time to look at it closely. Now she took the frame down and held it in front of her.

It was one of those studio portraits, with a Christmas background. Colton sat on a stool. A woman was nestled in front of him, Liam on her lap. Colton's wife. Her hair was a medium brown, the same color as her eyes. Though she wore makeup, it was understated. There was nothing striking about her individual features.

But she was gorgeous. She radiated warmth and friendliness, her easy smile an outward expression of inner joy. If one could deduce personality from a photograph, Mandy Gale was the type of person every woman wanted to have as a best friend. The world had lost someone special.

A key rattled in the front door lock and she set the frame back on the dresser feeling as if she'd almost been caught eavesdropping. Colton was home, with dinner. He'd called forty minutes ago to take her order.

She stepped into the kitchen as the door swung open. Colton held up two plastic bags. "Chinese takeout. Courtesy of China Town Buffet."

She drew in a fragrant breath. "Smells wonderful."

Colton carried the bags to the kitchen table. "How did everything go today?"

"Fine." He wasn't asking about *her* day. He was asking about Liam's. Colton Gale wasn't a man for small talk. "When I took him to day care, he went from me to his teacher without any fuss."

"Good."

He disappeared through the door behind him, then returned a minute later, holding Liam. By the time he had him strapped in to his high chair, she'd filled two water glasses and put milk in a sippy cup.

He removed the foam containers from the plastic bags. "I'm guessing there weren't any threats."

"No. Just like yesterday."

"Good."

He'd wanted her close but not conspicuous. Although he'd explained the situation to the owner of the day care, he didn't want to alarm the workers or the other parents. So she'd parked a short distance down the road and watched the activity through binoculars.

After laying a cellophane-wrapped package of plastic silverware at each place, Colton sat adjacent to his son at the four-person table, and Jasmine took the chair opposite Colton. Pleasant aromas wafted up from the container in front of her, and her stomach rumbled.

But she waited. She'd learned her first night there that the Gales never ate without saying grace.

Colton took his son's hand, then hers. The first time, he'd asked if she minded. She'd said no. Praying before meals was a sweet tradition.

When he bowed his head and began to pray, even Liam closed his eyes. Jasmine did, too, but only out of respect for the man sitting across from her. The God Colton worshipped was one she didn't like very much—an ever-present, all-powerful God who saw the suffering in the world but chose to ignore it. It was much less disturbing to imagine a distant God who set everything in motion, then turned His back to let nature take its course.

For the fourth night in a row, she listened to Colton thank God for His protection over them. *She* was the one providing the protection, but whatever.

When he finished his prayer, he tore into the cellophane package that held his plastic silverware and napkin. "I called a fencing contractor at lunchtime. I'm meeting him here at noon tomorrow."

"Good." The backyard was fenced, and that was currently where Brutus was. But the entire front was unguarded.

Colton continued in his professional no-nonsense tone. "They'll connect to the existing fence and take it all the way to the road. They told me if I go ahead with the contract tomorrow, they'll do the work this weekend."

"Good. Brutus is our first line of defense. It's best if he can access the entire yard."

Colton turned his attention to eating, all topics of business thoroughly covered. But the silence wasn't uncomfortable. Though they were all living under the same roof, Colton was keeping that professional distance.

That was fine with her. She wasn't any more interested in a relationship than he was. When the sting of her latest disaster finally faded and she was ready to put herself out there again, it certainly wouldn't be for a man who was still grieving the loss of his wife.

Frenzied barking from outside sent her into fight mode, and she sprang to her feet. From what she'd gathered, the dog didn't bark unless he had a reason to. Colton's clenched jaw and the lines of worry around his eyes confirmed her suspicions.

She retrieved a flashlight from the kitchen drawer and reached the back door the same time he did. He planted his hand against it, his other arm extended palm up for the flashlight. "I'll check it out."

"You need to stay inside. And keep away from the windows."

He bristled. He was probably used to being the protector, especially with women and children.

But that was the job he'd hired her to do. "I'm the one who's armed and wearing Kevlar."

His eyes narrowed. "You're supposed to stay with Liam."

"No, I'm supposed to *protect* Liam and, in the process, also protect you. Right now, there may be a threat out there. I'd suggest you let me go investigate."

His jaw was still tight, but he dropped his hand and gave her a sharp nod.

She opened the door enough to slip through. "Lock this behind me. Don't open it unless I give you an *all clear.*"

After a glance around, she stepped onto the back deck and drew her weapon. Dusk had passed and full night was fast approaching. Brutus was on the side of the house, to her right, still barking.

She crept that direction, dried leaves crunching beneath her feet. A chilly breeze cut right through her, and a shiver shook her shoulders. The light jacket she always wore hid her holster from view but offered little protection against the winter cold. She should have grabbed her coat.

When she rounded the corner, Brutus stood with his back to her, facing the front yard. He'd stopped barking, but deep growls rumbled in his chest, and his body rippled with tension.

A rustle sounded a few yards to the side of them, raising the fine hairs on the back of her neck. Every sense shot to full alert with the impending threat of an ambush.

She wasn't in Afghanistan anymore. But she didn't try to shake off the sensation. That state of being constantly on guard, trying to anticipate potential threats before they could become imminent, made her good at what she did.

She clicked on the flashlight and directed its beam into the woods. There was no sign of movement. Had she just heard the wind? Or was someone out there?

After stepping through the gate, she closed it behind her, then approached the tree line. Except for the rustle of leaves in the breeze and Brutus's low-pitched growls, the night was quiet.

She swept the beam back and forth, studying the ground in front of her. Light reflected against under-brush brown and dried after a couple of winter freezes.

Her hand stilled. At the edge of the woods, decaying growth was pressed down and lying against the ground. Someone had recently come through there.

Whoever it had been was likely long gone. He'd apparently come out of the woods, then run across the front yard, since that was the direction Brutus was looking when she'd first come out.

After making a final rotation with the flashlight, she walked back to the house. The key Colton had given her when they'd arrived was in her pocket. Instead of using it, she rapped on the door. "Let me in."

It swung inward moments later. As soon as she was safely inside, she spun on him. "I told you not to unlock the door unless I gave you an *all clear*."

"You did."

"No, I said 'let me in.' There's a difference. What if someone was holding a gun to my head?"

His lips pressed into a thin line. "Okay, I get it."

"In that case, you'd take Liam, run out a different way and pray to your God that no one sees you."

He sank into his chair, the weight of her words reflected on his face. "Did you see anything?"

"Someone came out of the woods and left through the front yard."

His eyebrows shot up. "You saw him?"

"No. The underbrush was pressed down. When I got to Brutus, he was staring into the front yard, growling."

She cast a glance at Liam, who was sitting at the table, munching on a rangoon, oblivious to the tension of the adults in the room.

Colton nodded. "It's possible it was nothing, some teenagers trying to make their way home by dark, not realizing this place is now occupied." He frowned, wrapping a protective arm around his son's shoulders. "Or maybe someone was checking to see how secure we are."

She took her seat opposite him, and he continued.

"We need to keep our guard up."

"No problem."

Her guard was always up. Night or day. Sleeping or awake.

Three years ago, she'd left behind the dangers of Afghanistan. But she'd swapped them for other threats, not as constant, but just as real.

If there was one thing Colton would never have to worry about, it was her state of readiness.

THREE

A single lamp burned in the living room, its glow not quite reaching the far corners of the space. The fire that had blazed in the fireplace earlier that evening had long since turned to ash.

Colton sat in the overstuffed chair, silent and alone. How many hours had Mandy occupied this exact spot, curled up in an afghan, an open book in her lap? This had been her favorite place to read.

Now he'd taken over her spot. Except his reading wasn't for pleasure. A bulging expandable folder sat on the end table next to him, and a bound document occupied his lap. It was the deposition of a store clerk held up at gunpoint.

He flipped the last page, then closed the plastic binder. When he'd slid it back into the expandable folder, he removed the next item for review.

Tomorrow was Friday, the end of his first week back at the Cherokee County district attorney's office. After almost losing his son, nothing could have kept him in Atlanta. But he'd been blessed that someone was leaving his old office and he'd been able to step immediately into a job. After his extended leave of absence, his savings account was reaching dangerously low levels.

He opened the next piece of discovery, then let his gaze drift to the front wall. Curtains covered all the lower windows, but beyond the edge of the hemlock outside, stars were visible through some of the high trapezoid-shaped windows.

Liam had been in bed for some time. So had Jasmine. Since it was nearing midnight, that was where he should be. Eventually he'd head there—when he was beyond exhaustion and the blessed oblivion of sleep was within reach.

God is in control. It was a fact he'd known since age fifteen. But for the past six months, he'd had to recite those four words again and again. Even more in the past week. Unfortunately, all the reminders didn't seem to penetrate those inner spaces where peace resided. His world had fallen apart, and he hadn't been able to regain his footing.

With a sigh, he lowered his eyes to the document in his lap. Sometime later, he stuffed the pages he'd been reading into the folder and rose from the chair. He couldn't say he'd reached the point of exhaustion, but if he stayed up much later, he'd be worthless tomorrow.

When he turned off the light, a faint glow shone from the partially open door off the side of the kitchen. Burning a night-light was the only way he could get Liam to sleep. If it bothered Jasmine, she hadn't mentioned it.

He padded silently in that direction, then paused at the open door. Liam lay in the small bed at the far side of the room, eyes closed and thumb in his mouth. A thin curtain of wispy blond hair had fallen over one side of his face. His mouth moved in a series of sucking motions, then again grew still.

Colton drew in a shaky breath. Love swelled inside him, mingled with a sadness that pierced his heart. He was trying his hardest to be both mother and father. But as he'd watched his little boy retreat further into himself, he'd known it wasn't enough.

He started to turn away, then hesitated. He'd wanted to keep Liam with him during the night, but Jasmine wouldn't hear of it. She'd said she wouldn't risk someone again tranquilizing the dog, then slipping in to whisk Liam away while she slept in another room. She was the security expert, so he'd given in, even though he didn't like it. Having his son sleeping on the opposite side of the house upset every protective instinct he possessed.

But *opposite side of the house* wasn't as bad as it sounded. The two bedroom doors were less than twenty feet apart, Liam's off the side of the kitchen, his off the opposite side of the living room. The house was also equipped with a security system now. According to Jasmine, Tri State had finished the installation at three that afternoon.

Poking his head into the room, he sought out the other bed, against the wall to his right. Jasmine was curled on her side, back toward the wall, blanket tucked under her chin. Instead of resting in its usual soft layers, her short hair jutted outward in disarray, as if she'd done some tossing and turning.

One hand lay near her face. But it wasn't relaxed and open. Instead, her fingers were curled into a fist. Even in sleep, she projected a tense readiness. Not good for her, but great for his son. And a huge comfort for him. Allowing Jasmine to be responsible for his son's safety had been a good choice.

He backed away and crept silently through the kitchen. It wouldn't do to have Jasmine awaken to find him staring at her. She'd probably think he was some kind of a creep. But it wasn't like that. He didn't think of her as anything more than his and Liam's bodyguard.

And he never would. The complete opposite of Mandy, she was so not his type. Where Mandy was soft and relaxed, Jasmine was hard and rigid. The warmth and openness that had always drawn him to Mandy seemed to be lacking in Jasmine. He'd never witnessed anything but cool professionalism. As far as openness, something told him she guarded her personal details like the Secret Service guarded the president.

When he stepped into his room, he left the door open. Ten minutes later, he was lying in bed, staring at the darkened ceiling. Another thirty minutes passed before sleep crept close enough to brush against consciousness. His thoughts slowed, growing more and more random.

A terror-filled wail split the silence. He stumbled from bed, heart in his throat. It took almost landing on his face to realize one foot was still tangled in the sheets. No matter how many times it happened, he'd never get used to Liam's middle-of-the-night screams. He'd hoped the intensity and frequency would lessen with time, but so far, they hadn't.

A second shriek set his teeth on edge. Then sobs followed, wails of sorrow rather than fear. He burst into Liam's room, flipping the switch as he passed. Stark white light obliterated every shadow.

He skidded to a stop. Liam's bed was empty. Jasmine had already scooped him up and sat in the wooden rocking chair. She held him tightly, his head resting against her chest. Her face was tilted downward as she whispered soothing words into his hair.

She glanced up, meeting Colton's gaze. Her eyes seemed to hold a lingering wildness of their own. Before he could analyze what he was seeing, she returned her attention to the sobbing boy in her lap.

Liam took a shuddering breath, then lifted one arm to partially circle her waist.

Colton clenched his fists. Jasmine shouldn't be the one comforting him. Mandy should. The boy needed his mother.

An inner voice told him he was being irrational. On some level he agreed. But he was powerless against the emotions bombarding him.

"I'll take him." His tone was stiff and cold.

Jasmine looked up again, her brows drawn together. When she tried to move Liam, his hand tightened around the fabric of her silk pajamas.

Colton reached for him. "Come here, buddy. Daddy's here."

Liam finally released his hold. When Colton took him, Liam's arms went around his neck. He eased himself down onto Jasmine's bed, since she was still occupying the rocking chair. Already, guilt was pricking him.

"I appreciate what you did for him." It probably hadn't been easy. Jasmine didn't seem like the gentle, motherly type.

"I didn't mind."

He owed her an apology, as well as an explanation. *Sorry I snapped at you. I was angry that you were here instead of my dead wife.*

Okay, maybe not.

"I'm sorry he woke you up." That was an apology. Sort of.

"I was already awake."

He wasn't surprised. When he'd checked on them, she hadn't looked to be in a sound sleep. At least not a relaxed one.

She looked away. "Nightmares are the pits, especially for kids."

Her words seemed to be more than an opinion. Her tone held a *been there, done that* sentiment.

He nodded. "They're pretty regular, have been ever since... For the past six months."

"Since your wife's death."

"Yeah." He shook his head. "It was sudden. Brain aneurysm. We had no time to prepare." Not that it would have done any good. No amount of preparation would lessen the blow of saying goodbye to one's soul mate.

"I'm sorry." Her eyes held the same sympathy he'd seen when they'd first arrived at the Murphy house. Not just sympathy. Empathy. Like she'd walked in his shoes. Or some that fit in a far too similar way.

"Thanks." He forced a smile, but only one side of his mouth cooperated. "I've tried to keep things as normal for Liam as possible." Normalcy when one's entire world had shifted wasn't easy to accomplish.

Actually, *normal* was gone. Trying to recapture the life they used to have was pointless. Instead, he was settling in to a new life, defining a new normal, while still holding on to the few constants. Though it was often the last thing he felt like doing, he'd continued with church, trips to the park and other activities Liam enjoyed, even during their stay in Montana.

Tomorrow would be the first Friday in December, the night of the Murphy Christmas Art Walk. The event had been one of his and Mandy's traditions and what kicked off the decorating they'd done at the Murphy house, even when they'd lived in Atlanta.

"Tomorrow night..." He started the thought aloud before he could change his mind. He wasn't kidding himself. Holidays were going to be pure torture. Getting through them would require every ounce of strength he possessed. "I'm taking Liam to the Christmas Art Walk. We'll need you to come along."

No way was he taking his son out without Jasmine's protection. Since arriving in Murphy, he'd felt safe, except for the incident two nights ago when Brutus had caught someone prowling around. Since nothing had happened since, it was probably just kids passing through.

Jasmine shrugged. "Sure. What's the Christmas Art Walk?"

"We stroll around downtown Murphy, where they have art, food, live music and, of course, the lighting of the tree in the square. We'll go out for supper first, my treat."

She gave a sharp nod. "Will do."

He rose and moved to his son's bed. As he and Jasmine had talked, Liam's arms had slowly slid from around his neck. He positioned the boy in his bed and tucked the stuffed rabbit into the crook of one elbow. Liam's other thumb slipped into his mouth.

Colton straightened and tilted his head toward his son. "His nightmares, they usually only happen once in any given night."

"No problem, even if it's more."

He left the room and headed toward his own. Tomorrow night, he'd be tackling the first of their Christmas traditions.

Same time, same event, same location. There'd even be three of them, like before. But instead of Mandy, Jasmine would be with them.

It just wasn't right.

But they weren't a family unit, not the three of them. They were a father and son with their bodyguard. He wasn't even trying to pretend there was anything more.

It still somehow felt all wrong.

* * *

Jasmine stood in Hiwassee Valley rec center's playground, straight-legged jeans disappearing into the tops of her boots and her jacket hiding both her weapon and her Kevlar vest. Liam sat in one of the swings, fists clutching the chains as she pushed him. He was dressed the same as she was, minus the vest and in tennis shoes instead of boots. Heavier coats waited for them in the car. When the sun went down, they'd need them. Right now, the temperature was pleasant.

Colton had called an hour ago with a change of plans. They were still doing supper and the Christmas Art Walk, but he wouldn't make it home first. So he'd asked her to meet him at five at the Cherokee County Courthouse downtown. Since she was running early, the park offered a fun detour. Maybe it would not only distract Liam for a short time but also wear him out enough to sleep well tonight.

"Would you like to try out the slide?" Though Liam didn't respond, she brought him to a slow stop and lifted him from the swing.

Colton had apologized for him disturbing her sleep. In actuality, he hadn't. She'd awoken from a nightmare herself shortly before he'd started screaming. When she'd scooped him up, she'd still been shaking from her own private terrors.

Then something unexpected had happened. As she'd held and soothed him, an odd sense of comfort had woven through her, shattering the images flashing in her mind and calming her spinning thoughts. The whole experience had caught her off guard. She didn't seek comfort from anyone. She dealt with everything on her own.

As a child, she'd had no choice. Often, she'd been left alone while her mother partied through the night. Or her mother left her with random people for days on end. Most didn't want to be bothered. Some did, men who tried to do things she didn't understand but somehow sensed were wrong.

As an adult, keeping herself closed off had been a hard habit to break. She'd even been tight-lipped with the counselors the army had assigned to help her process the horrors she'd seen and adjust to civilian life.

She led Liam to one of the slides, searching the perimeter as she'd been doing since they arrived fifteen minutes ago. Nothing raised any red flags. Several moms and a couple of dads stood or sat on benches. Jasmine had already matched the adults to their charges.

She was just finishing her three-hundred-sixty-degree observation when something over her left shoulder snagged her gaze. A man stood under the pavilion outside the fence, leaning against one of the posts, watching the activity on the playground. Was he one of those creeps who liked to hang out where young children played? Or was he interested in one child in particular?

Liam climbed the stairs, and she moved around to the base of the slide, keeping the man in her peripheral vision. He continued to watch. The fine hairs on the back of her neck stood up.

She shifted position, the weight of her weapon in its holster now more pronounced against her hip. She likely wouldn't have to draw it. If the man represented any kind of threat, he'd be crazy to act in a public place in broad daylight.

When it came time to leave, he hadn't moved. Liam walked with her to the Suburban without any objection. As she pulled into the courthouse parking lot, her phone buzzed with an incoming text. Colton was finished. Perfect timing. Two or three minutes later, he approached the passenger side, and she lowered the window.

He leaned inside. "Are you okay with taking your vehicle, or shall we transfer the car seat?"

"I can drive. Hop in."

He directed her through a turn onto Valley River Avenue. The art walk appeared to be in full swing, with every parking space occupied and people roaming the sidewalks. An alleyway between two buildings opened up into a parking area. If Colton hadn't been with her, she'd have never found it.

When they'd walked back to the front of the building, a sign overhead announced The Daily Grind.

She looked up at Colton. "A coffee shop?"

"And more. Salads, soups and sandwiches. Fast, but good. One of the favorite places around for people to congregate."

He opened the door, then walked in behind her, carrying Liam. In front of her, a wide hallway separated the Curiosity Shop Bookstore on the right from The Daily Grind on the left. They joined the end of a short line. Above and behind those working the counter, the menu was displayed on boards. She decided on a grilled panini sandwich with hot roast beef and Swiss.

After placing their orders, they found an empty table at the front. Colton positioned Liam in a booster seat and took the chair next to him. Jasmine sat opposite them. Large windows offered a clear view of Valley River Avenue. People strolled by just outside.

Jasmine shifted her attention to Colton. "Are you working tomorrow?"

"Not at the office, but I did put some files in my vehicle before walking over to where you'd parked."

"Are you always this much of a workaholic?"

He shrugged. "I've got a lot of catching up to do. I'm taking over someone else's caseload."

She nodded, even though he hadn't answered her question. She glanced around the interior space, then looked out the window again. A group of people had stopped to converse, blocking her view of anything beyond.

After they moved on, she scanned the area. The sun had set, and the last rays of light were fading. Her gaze fell on a figure across the street, and she tensed. Shadows hid his face, but the baseball cap, jeans and bulky coat matched the clothing of the man at the playground.

"Is everything okay?"

Colton's words pulled her attention back inside. For a nonmilitary, nonsecurity guy, he was pretty observant.

She cast a glance back out the window. The guy was gone.

"Everything's fine." She wouldn't alarm him yet. Based on what she'd seen, most of Murphy turned out for this event. The man across the street might not even be the same person. If he was, he hadn't followed her. She'd been watching too closely.

When they finished eating, Colton looked at his watch. "If we want to make it to the tree lighting, we'll have to walk fast."

"I'm up for it if you are." She stood. "So, what happens at the tree lighting? Other than lighting the tree."

"There's children's music and dance and a kids' jingle bell walk. Then Santa arrives on a fire truck."

"Sounds like fun."

Especially for a kid. She hoped Liam would enjoy it. She would have at that age. If the small town she grew up in had had activities like that, she hadn't known about them.

Her mother apparently had, at least the adult parties.

More than once Jasmine had gotten up in the morning to find that her mother had come in during the night and passed out on the living room floor still wearing a Christmas hat.

When they reached the town square, a good-size crowd was already gathered. Jasmine scanned those standing around, searching for the man she'd seen at the park. Throughout each activity, she continued to look. If he was there, he was staying hidden.

When the last activity ended, Colton shifted his son to his other hip. Liam didn't participate in the jingle bell walk with the other kids, but his eyes were alert, taking in everything that was going on around him. Maybe next year.

Of course, she wouldn't be there to witness it.

An unexpected sense of loss settled in her core. She mentally shook herself. Being part of a real family, albeit temporarily, was messing with her. She had no intention of putting down any kind of roots. She loved the transient nature of what she did. The crazy pace helped her stay ahead of the memories.

Unfortunately, the nightmares always managed to catch up with her. No matter what she'd done or where she'd gone, she had never gotten rid of them. After years of fighting, all she'd managed to do was trade childhood terrors for adult-size ones.

As the crowd began to spread out, Colton moved down the sidewalk. "Now for the art walk."

For some time, they wandered in and out of the shops. Several stores down, a variety of paintings were on display. The artist sat to the side. Jasmine stopped to watch as the woman dipped a brush into one of the globs of paint on her palette, then spread it with sure strokes onto the canvas in front of her.

It looked like a local scene, as did the others around the room. This one was a park with mountains in the background, silhouetted against a striking sunset.

Jasmine stepped away to look at the other paintings more closely. "I've always envied artistic people. I never progressed past Paint by Numbers."

Colton stood next to her. "Mandy painted, watercolor."

"Your wife." Colton hadn't mentioned her name previously, but Gunn had.

"Yeah. She did it as a hobby, but she was good."

So Liam's mother wasn't just loved and needed. She was talented, too. With so many rotten people walking around, why did someone like Mandy Gale have to die? Why did any good people die young? Men and women serving their country, sent home in caskets. What kind of God made those decisions?

When she reached the door, bluegrass music drifted to her from somewhere nearby, probably a local band entertaining the attendees. She stepped out onto the sidewalk, glancing up and down the street.

A man stood about twenty feet away, the glow of a streetlamp spilling over him. The bill of his cap cast his face in shadow, but this time she was sure. It was the man from the park.

She reached for her phone. "Pick up Liam. I want to take your picture."

When he'd done as she asked, she turned the phone sideways and touched the screen, focusing on the figure to the right. After snapping three pictures, she scrolled through them.

Colton peered over her shoulder. "Usually it's better to center the subjects you're taking a picture of. You got Liam, but you cut me in half. I'm glad you're a better bodyguard than photographer."

She ignored his teasing criticism and expanded the picture, moving it to the side until a grainy face occupied the center of the screen.

"Do you recognize this man?"

"No, why?" His eyes lit with understanding, then respect. "Who is he?"

She looked back toward the streetlight. As expected, the man was gone.

"I was hoping you could tell me. I took Liam to the park before meeting you. I noticed him standing some distance away, watching the activity on the playground."

"And you saw him when we were in the Grind." It was a statement rather than a question.

"I wasn't sure. He was across the street, in shadow. But when I saw him this time, I knew it was the same guy. Are you sure you've never seen him?"

He looked at the picture again. "It's hard to tell. His face is dark."

Yeah, the shadows were even more pronounced than what she'd seen. Maybe the authorities could enhance the photos enough to identify him.

She shrank the picture until the man's full length displayed on the screen. "Could he be one of the guys who tried to take Liam?"

Colton studied the image. "I didn't see their faces, but this could be the thinner guy."

She pocketed the phone. Maybe he *was* one of the kidnappers. Or maybe he was just a Murphy resident who liked to hang out at the park and attend the town's activities.

But that wasn't what her gut told her. She'd gotten icky vibes all three times she'd seen him.

When she looked up at Colton, his jaw was tight and

his lips were compressed into a thin line. "Are you dead set on finishing the art walk?"

"No."

"Good."

Because if there was one thing she'd learned over the years, it was to always listen to her instincts.

FOUR

Colton hauled a large empty box out of the middle of the living room and stood it against the wall. Jasmine sat on the rug, back against the coffee table, piles of plastic branches surrounding her.

Walmart bags lined the couch. Liam had pulled boxes of Christmas lights out of one and set them on the floor. Now he was tackling a second bag, pulling out ornaments. At least he was engaged. Maybe he was even enjoying himself.

Colton lowered himself to the floor and assembled the tree stand. He and Mandy had always had a live tree. This year's would be artificial. And though the attic held boxes of decorations, he wouldn't use them. He was committed to making Christmas meaningful for Liam, but he didn't have to let each strand of garland, every ornament, even the fresh pine scent of a live tree, be a reminder of what he'd lost.

Last night, he'd barely gotten through the activities in town. Cutting out early had been a relief, both to escape possible danger and to no longer have to pretend he was having a great time when he was dying inside.

Jasmine unfolded a piece of paper and smoothed out

the creases against the coffee table. "Okay, bottom row, blue." She passed him a handful of branches.

Colton smiled. "So, you're a follow-the-directions kind of girl."

"Yeah. Saves time in the long run."

His thoughts exactly. "Someone needs to explain that to my brother. Step-by-step instructions feel too much like structure, something he avoids like Black Death."

"And you're a by-the-book guy."

"Totally." One year, a church had taken on his group home as a project and bought every child a Christmas gift. He and Cade had received model cars. Cade had finished his in half the time, but some of the components never made it into the car because he'd glued together the exterior before finishing the inside. Cade was bright, but an innate impulsiveness had gotten him into trouble more than once.

Jasmine nodded. "Didn't take me long to pick up on the fact you guys are polar opposites."

The tree took form as they progressed up the inner pole, each series of branches shorter than the last. Liam stayed busy with the contents of the bags. Across the room, Brutus lay against the wall, silently watching the activity.

The guys from Western Carolina Fence had arrived that morning and were still hard at work. The dog hadn't been happy to have strangers tromping around his yard. Keeping him inside was less stressful, all the way around.

When they finished assembling the tree, Colton stepped back. "Now for the lights."

He retrieved a box from the haphazard stack against the couch. Liam handed him an ornament, still in its packaging, a teddy bear holding a bouquet of candy canes.

"You like this one?"

Liam's mouth curved in a small smile, and Colton swallowed around a sudden lump in his throat. *Thank You, Lord.* It was just a smile, one minuscule step on the path back to the happy child he used to be. But every bit of progress, no matter how small, felt like cause for celebration.

And he'd do whatever it took to see the progress continue. He'd keep up the cheery front. He'd gotten good at stuffing the grief beneath layers of *I've got it all together* for the benefit of his son.

He knelt in front of Liam and placed the ornament on the coffee table. "The lights have to go on first, then the garland. How about if you get the rest of the ornaments out and put them with this one?"

Liam nodded and went to work tackling the task he'd been given. By the time Colton had placed the last strand of lights, boxes of ornaments were spread across the coffee table. Garland went on next, while Liam watched.

Colton crouched at the table in front of his son. "Now the ornaments."

Another smile, this one a little bigger. It tugged a matching one out of Colton. They'd been back in Murphy for one week, and already he was seeing his son slowly reengage with his world. The move had been a good choice, one he'd never have considered if not for the events of last week.

Another thought slid through the back of his mind, the fact that the move to Murphy wasn't the only change in his son's life. There was also Jasmine's presence.

He didn't want to credit any of Liam's progress to her being there. She was a temporary addition to their lives. If Liam became too attached, his behavior would revert right back once she left.

He scooped up his son, a sense of protectiveness surging through him. Somehow, he'd make sure that didn't happen. "We'll let Miss Jasmine put the hooks on them, and you can hang them."

After tearing into the perforated back of the package, Jasmine removed a handful of wire hooks and laid them on the coffee table. One by one, she affixed them to the ornaments and handed them to Liam. Colton held him up to adorn the higher branches, gradually working their way around and down the tree.

Each time Liam placed ornaments side by side, Colton let them be. He wasn't going for perfection. Everything he was doing was for his son's benefit. And Liam didn't care that the decorations weren't evenly spaced. Although he didn't say a word, several spontaneous smiles revealed how much he was enjoying himself.

Jasmine was smiling, too. But the spontaneity Liam displayed was lacking in her. Now that she wasn't task-focused, her features held tightness. He wasn't the only one feigning enthusiasm.

He placed Liam on the floor. After directing him to one of the lower branches, he glanced up at Jasmine. "You seem to be trying as hard as I am."

She didn't have to ask him what he meant, confirmation he'd pegged her right. Instead, she shrugged. "I've never made a big deal out of Christmas. As a child, I was forgotten. As an adult, I don't see the purpose. That whole 'peace on earth, goodwill to men' message is nothing but a pipe dream."

"And I thought *I* was jaded."

She shrugged again but didn't comment.

"How about you?" She swept her hand toward the newly decorated tree. "Is this how you grew up?"

"Till age seven and from age fifteen forward. Between

seven and fifteen, how I celebrated Christmas depended on what foster or group home I was in."

She lifted her brows. "You were in foster care?"

"For a while. The Gales adopted me when I was fifteen."

"What happened to your birth parents?"

"My mom died." When he was seven, the breast cancer she'd defeated three years earlier came back with a vengeance. Six months later, she was gone. "What happened to my dad is anybody's guess. They divorced when I was young."

What he said was true, but there was more to the story. He and Cade had both ended up with their father. But after he'd left them alone too many times, Child Protective Services had stepped in, and they'd landed in foster care. Though the state worked with his father, he never did get his act together and eventually signed away his parental rights.

She handed Liam another ornament. "That had to have been rough."

Colton met her gaze, and the words he was going to say stuck in his throat. He'd seen it again—that empathy, the silent message that said she'd been there. Close enough to understand, anyway.

He shrugged. "It was rough. But Cade and I at least got adopted. My friend Tanner aged out of the system. A lot of teenagers do."

"They kept you and Cade together?"

"Through foster care, they did. They tried to get us adopted together, but there weren't many adoptive parents up to the task of handling two messed-up boys, one brooding, angry and destructive, and the other with a mischievous streak a mile wide."

She gave him a wry smile. "Let me guess who was who."

He returned her smile. "Pretty obvious, huh? Although, I think I've obliterated any destructive tendencies. And anger isn't so much an issue anymore, either." He pursed his lips. "As far as Cade's mischievousness...that just manifests itself in other ways now."

"You were adopted separately? But you have the same last name."

"Another family started adoption proceedings for Cade." The more serious, studious twin, Colton had always been a little envious of his outgoing, carefree brother. When Cade went to a permanent home at age fourteen, that slight envy became full-blown jealousy.

"A week before the adoption would have been final, the adoptive parents backed out."

Jasmine's eyes widened. "How awful."

"The family realized the charming, fun-loving personality that had drawn them in came with some characteristics that weren't so pleasant, especially when the police got involved."

Cade had seemed to handle the rejection well. But Colton knew better. After that, his brother's mischievousness and impulsiveness sometimes bordered on self-destruction.

"I'd already gone to the Gales by that time, so that made things worse for him. But once my adoption was final, the Gales adopted Cade, too."

She threaded a hook into the last ornament and handed it to Liam. "They must be amazing people." The wistfulness in her tone left Colton wondering what had been missing from her own childhood.

"They are." He'd never seen two finer examples of Christians. "They were in the process of making retirement plans when my grandfather was diagnosed with Alzheimer's and my grandmother had a stroke. So a year ago, they put their travel plans on hold and moved to upper New York to care for my grandparents."

Liam raised his arms toward Jasmine. The softest whisper reached Colton's ears.

His pulse kicked into overdrive. "Did he just say something?"

"I think he said 'more.'"

Colton scooped him up and spun him around, heart still pounding. "You want more? Sorry, buddy, you hung them all up."

Liam's thumb went into his mouth, but the vacancy Colton had grown accustomed to seeing in his eyes wasn't there. Instead, they sparked with life. He moved to the couch and sat, positioning his son on his lap facing the tree. "You did such a good job. That's the prettiest Christmas tree ever."

The thumb came out, and Liam pointed toward the tree. Colton's heart sang. If the smile had been a small step, the single word had been a giant leap.

When he shifted his gaze to Jasmine, she was watching him. For one unguarded moment, he saw in her eyes the same wistfulness he'd heard in her tone. But there was something else, too. Longing. It threaded a path right to his heart.

The next moment, it was gone, hidden behind that veil of self-sufficiency that seemed to always cloak her. She moved to the front window next to the tree and pulled the drapes aside. "They've got the posts and top rail up and are starting to run the fence."

"Good." He tamped down whatever it was he'd felt moments earlier. Her rotten childhood, the traumas she'd faced as an adult—they were none of his business. Just as his personal struggles were none of hers.

He joined her at the window. He didn't envy the men their job. Mixed in with the rich topsoil and clay were varying sizes of rocks. Lots of them. He'd learned that when Mandy had wanted decorative ornamentals planted around the house. Of course, the men currently working outside were professionals and far better equipped than he'd been.

The ringtone sounded on his phone. The screen displayed a familiar number. He swiped it and greeted his brother.

Static interrupted Cade's voice. "I've wanted...several times...insane hour."

Colton stepped outside, even though the problem was likely on Cade's end. "Where are you?"

"Egypt...driving...Cairo."

"Your satellite cell service stinks."

"Hold on."

Colton waited. When Cade came back on, the background noise he'd heard earlier was gone. So was the majority of the static.

"That's much better." He'd apparently stopped, maybe even gotten out of the vehicle and climbed a hill. If the area surrounding Cairo had hills. Colton wouldn't know. His brother was the world traveler.

"I've wanted to call several times, but it's always been some insane hour in the States. Are you and Liam okay?"

He leaned against the deck railing. "We're fine. We've had a couple of small scares, but nothing came of them."

"What kind of scares?" Worry laced Cade's tone, strongly enough that the thousands of miles separating them didn't dilute it.

"Someone cutting across the yard, which we decided was probably a teenager from the neighborhood."

"And?"

"And someone hanging out near the park yesterday afternoon and the Christmas Art Walk last night. I don't think he posed any threat." No sense in saying otherwise. None of this was Cade's deal. Half a world away, he couldn't do anything about it anyway.

"You've got to stay away from Atlanta."

Colton lifted his brows at the urgency in his brother's tone. His philosophy in life had always been "Nothing's gonna happen." Apparently, he wasn't so optimistic when his nephew's safety was at stake.

"Trust me, I'm not going anywhere near there until whoever tried to take Liam has been locked up."

"Good." Cade heaved a sigh of relief. "You know, I already miss the little guy."

"Look at the bright side. There's no one to spill juice all over you."

Cade's laughter held a heavy dose of affection. "Would you believe I even miss the mishaps?"

The last mishap had given Cade a lot more time with his nephew than he'd planned. The evening before the break-in and attempted kidnapping, Cade had stopped by for dinner, then ended up spending the night after Liam had loosened the top on his sippy cup and spilled the entire contents over him. Colton had loaned him some sweats and thrown both shirt and pants into the washer before the red juice could leave a stain.

Cade continued, his tone turning from playful to eager. "So how are things progressing with the hot bodyguard? It's been a week. I hope you've moved from the protector/protectee relationship to something much more interesting."

Colton groaned. After his meeting at Burch Security Specialists, he'd filled Cade in on the fact that his pretty neighbor was going to be the one providing the bodyguard services. Maybe he should have kept that detail to himself.

"Our relationship is strictly professional, as it will remain."

Sure, he admired her. Although she hadn't elaborated, she'd provided enough hints for him to know she hadn't had an easy life. But she'd survived whatever rough upbringing she'd had. Not just survived. Overcome.

She was strong, physically and emotionally. She'd risked her life serving her country and continued putting herself in danger serving those she protected. But she had no problem setting aside that strength and toughness to comfort a frightened little boy.

Yeah, he admired her. But that was as far as it would go. From what he'd gathered, Jasmine wasn't any more in the market for a relationship than he was.

Cade heaved a sigh. "Whatever. But I think you're passing up a golden opportunity."

When Colton didn't respond, Cade let the subject drop. "I've got to get to an appointment." The same urgency entered his tone. "No matter what, don't go back home. You've got to stay in Murphy. You hear me?"

"Yeah, loud and clear." Something dark fell over him, drawing his stomach into a knot. "What aren't you telling me?"

"I'm just worried. Somebody's threatening my nephew. Stay away from Atlanta. Lie low. Keep Jasmine close, Liam closer." A hum came through the phone. Cade had apparently gotten back in the car and cranked the engine. "I'll call you in a couple days."

The line went dead. Colton looked at his phone, brows dipping together. What was up with his brother? He never stressed about anything, even when stress was warranted. He took the adage "Don't worry, be happy" to extremes.

But no one had ever threatened Liam before. Cade obviously wasn't handling it any better than Colton was. Colton wasn't surprised. He and his brother were close, in spite of their differences. But if not for Cade's desire to talk to his nephew every week or two, the adults' interactions wouldn't be nearly as frequent.

He pushed himself away from the railing. The men were unrolling chain-link fence, affixing it to the framework they'd already installed. By the end of the day, they'd be finished. Brutus would be back outside with free run of the entire yard. Anyone trying to approach the house would find himself with a bite-size chunk taken out of his rear end.

The thought brought him some comfort. But not enough to soothe the lingering anxiety that still coursed through him.

He stepped back inside, where Liam was stuffing empty ornament boxes into a bag that Jasmine held open. A few minutes earlier, the sight would have warmed him. But a cold knot of worry had settled in his chest.

He didn't plan to go back to Atlanta anyway. But Cade's dire warnings had shaken him.

Was Cade afraid that if they returned, the kidnappers would try again? Or was it more than that?

Maybe someone got to him. Maybe before Cade left town, the kidnappers made some kind of threat.

And Cade was trying to protect him, to keep him from worrying.

It wasn't working.

Unfortunately, Cade's silence was doing just the opposite.

Jasmine fought the urge to retch. There was smoke, dust, screams.

And blood. So much blood.

Zach lay on the ground, clutching his stomach, his wails fraying her nerves. She added her own hands to the gaping wound, trying to help stanch the stream of blood. It didn't help. The river kept flowing, warm and sticky.

She'd been standing in front of him moments earlier. They'd kissed goodbye, then walked opposite directions to get ready to report for duty.

Then there was a shout of warning and the sound that struck terror deep into the core of every soldier—the whistle of an incoming mortar round. The nearby blast knocked her to the ground. When she'd gathered her wits enough to rise and search for Zach, the scene before her was what she'd found.

"Hang on, Zach. Help's coming."

But it was hopeless. She'd encountered Death enough times to know when it had gone from crouching at the door to leaping over the threshold.

Zach went suddenly still, eyes no longer focused. She opened her mouth, her own wail traveling up her throat. A warning sounded deep in her subconscious, and she squeezed off the scream.

A hand gripped her shoulder, and what she'd stifled moments earlier found full release.

"Shh, Jasmine. It's okay. You're safe."

Zach! She snapped her eyes open with a gasp.

But Zach wasn't there. She was no longer at the post in Afghanistan, chaos all around her, the stench of fear and death. She was in Liam's bedroom, his father standing over her.

"What are you doing in here?" Her tone was shrill and laced with panic, partly from the remnants of the nightmare, partly from the thought that Colton had been able to walk into the room and approach her bed without her knowing.

Nearby, Liam rolled over. She tried to sit up, but she was restrained. Fresh panic surged through her. She worked a hand free and heaved a sigh of relief. It was just the sheet and blanket. One side was still tucked between the mattress and box springs, the rest wound tightly around her.

Colton helped to pull the bedding from under her. "I was having trouble sleeping." His tone was low, soothing. The glow of the night-light washed over him, softening his features. "I went to the kitchen to get a drink and heard you thrashing around."

She pushed herself to an upright position as Liam started to cry. Colton moved that direction, and she sprang to her feet.

"Let me get him." It was only fair.

"You're not his babysitter."

"I'm the one who woke him up. Besides, it's Monday, the start of a new week. You need your sleep."

She scooped Liam from his bed. In a matter of seconds, he'd worked himself up to a full wail. She settled herself in the rocking chair, his legs draped over her right thigh. He calmed down and snuggled against her, thumb in his mouth.

As she rocked him, she rubbed his back, making slow circles with her palm. He drew in several shuddering breaths, then lifted his other arm to grip her silk pajamas.

She closed her eyes, letting her pulse slow and the images fade. Something cleansing washed over her, leaving behind an odd sense of calm. How could the comfort she tried to give flow both ways? How could the act of soothing Liam's fears be a balm for her own?

"What did you dream?"

The question jarred her eyes open. "Nothing important, just a nightmare."

"From your military days?"

He sat on her bed, fingers intertwined in his lap. Great. He was planning to stay awhile.

"Yeah." If he expected her to elaborate, he was going to be disappointed. She didn't discuss the memories that haunted her with anyone.

"You want to talk about it?"

"No." He wasn't her counselor.

But she *was* tasked with protecting his son. He needed to know that she wasn't in danger of flipping out and hurting Liam.

She drew in a stabilizing breath. "I've been out of the army for three years, living a fairly normal life. The horror of combat is behind me."

Sort of. The things she witnessed would never go away. But the nightmares had gradually decreased in frequency. More important, she was getting better at waking herself up before reaching the state that had drawn Colton into the room.

Not all her assignments had been in war zones. Only two had. During those deployments, she'd witnessed dozens of deaths. Every one of them had bothered her. Zach's had almost killed her. Their relationship hadn't been perfect. But it had been less dysfunctional than her previous ones.

Colton nodded. "If you ever want to talk about it, I'm a good listener."

"Thanks." But that wasn't how she did things.

He dipped his head toward his son. "Looks like he might be going back to sleep."

"I think you're right." Except for the occasional shuddering breath, he hadn't moved in several minutes.

Colton rose. "I'm going to take you up on your offer to let me get some sleep."

As she watched him walk from the room, tenderness wove through her. In spite of all of her toughness, sad stories got to her. And his was tragic on so many levels.

Suffering the death of his mother at age seven. Unwanted by his father. Bounced between foster and group homes for the next eight years. Left behind when his brother was adopted.

He'd overcome all of it, then had his family shattered again when his wife died. If anyone had grounds for claiming life wasn't fair, it was Colton.

But he didn't. During quiet times, he projected a sense of grief that was almost palpable. But an unexplainable peace seemed to run beneath it.

If she asked him about the peace he seemed to possess, he'd probably credit his faith in God. That didn't make sense, either. If Colton believed God was close enough to provide any type of comfort, he'd also have to believe that God was close enough to see what was happening and intervene.

Liam released a soft sigh, and his hand fell to his lap. He was fully asleep. She could lay him in his bed and return to her own.

Instead, she sat for a few more minutes, relishing his warmth against her and letting the soothing movement of the rocker continue to relax her. She tipped her face downward and pressed a soft kiss to the top of his head. Colton didn't want his son getting attached to her. He didn't express any concerns about her getting attached to the little boy.

Finally, she rose and laid him in his bed next to the stuffed rabbit. The thumb that had fallen out of his mouth went back in.

Her chest squeezed. Every child should be loved and cherished like Liam. Instead, too many grew up like her and Liam's father—unwanted, shuffled from place to place, fed but not nourished, cared for but not loved. Maybe Colton didn't feel life was unfair, but she certainly did.

She moved to her bed and crawled between the rumpled sheets. Watching Colton hold Liam Saturday, praising him for the job he'd done decorating the tree, had stirred something in her. It was something she desperately wanted, a longing she didn't even know she'd had.

It wasn't that she wanted it with Colton. Or even his sad, sweet little boy. She just wanted it. Period. That sense of home. Family. Maybe she'd find it eventually.

But not with Colton. The last thing she wanted to do was to try to step into the shoes of his dead wife. She'd never measure up to those standards.

Amazing mother. Loving wife. Artistic, talented and creative. Beautiful inside and out.

No way could she compete with that.

She wouldn't even try.

FIVE

Colton walked from the courthouse into late dusk. The parking lot lights and streetlights along Alpine had already come on.

As he made his way toward his vehicle, he scanned the area. There hadn't been any possible threats since the art walk a week ago, but he couldn't bring himself to fully relax. If life continued to be safe and uneventful, though, he'd have to eventually let Jasmine go. He couldn't afford to keep her on indefinitely.

In the meantime, her presence was a comfort, and not just for the security she provided. She was at least partially responsible for the improvement he was seeing in Liam.

Over the past week, several more words had slipped from his mouth. No full sentences, yet. He was still a long way from the chatty little boy he used to be. But it was a start.

Colton's cell phone vibrated at his side. A second, then third buzz told him it was a call rather than a text. Not Cade again. He was starting to sound like an audio clip on automatic replay. He'd called twice this week, and Colton had had to reassure him both times that he and Liam weren't going back to Atlanta, even for a brief visit.

He removed his phone from its clip, shaking his head. He was still trying to get used to the mature, somber side of Cade. When he swiped the screen, though, it wasn't his brother's name and number there.

Colton smiled. He and Doug Blanton hadn't just worked together since Colton's return to Atlanta. They'd gone to the same church and become good friends over the past couple of years.

Doug's booming voice came through the phone. "How is Murphy?"

"Good."

"No kidnappers or creepy stalker dudes?"

Doug knew the reasons behind the sudden move. Colton had caught up with him when he'd gone into the office to resign his position.

"Nope. Just a couple of false alarms." He pressed the key fob and approached the Highlander. Beyond its nose, a chain-link fence marked the edge of the parking lot, the guardrail inside an extra layer of protection from the ten- or twelve-foot drop-off to the road. "I did hire a bodyguard."

"That makes me feel better. Is he out of Atlanta?"

"Yeah, Burch Security. But it's a she rather than a he."

"Good." That fact obviously didn't bother Doug like it had him at first. Of course, it didn't bother him anymore. God had a way of placing people exactly where they needed to be.

As Doug caught him up on happenings around the DA's office, Colton settled into the driver's seat. Something white snagged his gaze—a sheet of paper tucked under the right wiper blade.

Uneasiness settled over him, and he shook it off. Kidnappers didn't leave notes on windshields. It was probably a flyer from one of the local businesses. He just needed to remove it before he pulled from the parking lot.

After ending the call a few minutes later, he stepped out to retrieve the page. As soon as he unfolded it, a bolt of panic shot up his spine. The paper fluttered to the ground. Bold, dark letters screamed out their message— *You can run, but you can't hide.*

His heart pounded, sending blood roaring through his ears. The men he fled from in Atlanta had found him. They knew where he worked. They probably also knew where he lived.

He had to warn Jasmine.

He bent to pick up the paper at the same time a shot rang out. Glass shattered, and he hit the pavement, face-down, heart pounding.

As he retrieved his phone and dialed 911, his thoughts spun. If his enemy was here in town, firing on him, that meant he wasn't at the house threatening his son.

Unless he'd gone there first.

The dispatcher picked up before the last thought could lodge too deeply. As he filled her in on what had happened, he doubled back to collect the paper, staying in a crouch. The light breeze had carried it across an empty parking space and pressed it against a car's tire two spaces over.

Handling just the corner, he picked it up and carried it to his vehicle. The bullet had entered the driver side of the windshield and exited the rear passenger window. Judging from the angle, it had likely come from the direction of the library. The trees lining that side of the road would have offered a handy place for a shooter to hide.

As soon as he ended the call, he brought up Jasmine's number. Sirens sounded nearby. Right downtown, he'd expected as much.

When the call went straight to voice mail, his stomach tightened. Why didn't she have her phone on? The sirens were moving closer. Maybe he should ask the police to dispatch another unit to his house.

Or maybe he had a better idea. It would take the police a good ten minutes to get there, but his friend Bryce lived one street over, on Ranger Road. Tanner lived a mile farther, on 294. Both worked in law enforcement, Tanner with Murphy PD and Bryce with Cherokee County.

Bryce answered on the second ring. He was on duty several miles the opposite direction. Colton ended the call without an explanation and brought up Tanner's number. A police cruiser turned onto Peachtree as his friend answered.

Colton dispensed with the formalities. "Where are you?"

"At Ingles, tackling the grocery list Paige texted me. Why?"

"I was going to have you check on Jasmine and Liam. Someone just shot at me, and I can't get ahold of her."

"Call 911."

"I have."

"I'm leaving my cart."

"No, go ahead and finish your shopping." Even if Tanner left the store immediately, he wouldn't make it to Colton's house until long after the on-duty officers arrived.

"On second thought, how about stopping by the courthouse and giving me a ride home?" His vehicle was evidence. He'd probably have to leave it there for some time.

As he disconnected the call, the cruiser made its way up the narrow drive into the courthouse parking lot. Its siren fell silent, but others still sounded nearby. Probably units searching for the shooter.

Before the officer could exit, Colton stepped up to his

open door. "Will you please send a unit to my house?" He rattled off the address. "With this attack on me, I'm worried about my son and his bodyguard."

The officer raised a brow but immediately reached for his radio. As he spoke, a little of Colton's tension eased. A unit would be dispatched from Cherokee County. When the officer finished, he turned his attention to Colton. "Show me where you were and where this shot came from."

Colton walked to his vehicle and relayed everything as it had happened. After donning latex gloves he'd retrieved from the car, the officer took the note into evidence.

"Any idea who'd want to take a shot at you?"

"I've made a few enemies during my time as an assistant DA." He gave the officer the same names he'd given Gunter Burch two weeks ago.

"Did you see or hear anything before the shot was fired? A vehicle speeding by or anything?"

"No. But it seemed to have come from over there." He nodded toward the library. Though it wasn't situated as high as the courthouse, its grounds sloped upward from the road. Not an ideal position, but doable.

He continued. "I didn't notice anything suspicious. But I'd just found the note, and I was pretty shaken. Someone tried to kidnap my son two weeks ago in Atlanta, so I came up here. The note tells me they've found me."

He shifted his weight, impatience tightening his shoulders. He needed to get home and check on Liam and Jasmine.

He drew in a steadying breath. Law enforcement was already on its way and would likely arrive within minutes. Meanwhile, he'd left Liam in Jasmine's care. She was sharp. She never let down her guard.

God, please protect them both.

A Silverado pickup pulled into one of the streetside parking spaces below, Tanner at the wheel. As he drew to a stop, the officer's radio came to life.

"The woman and child on Hilltop are unharmed."

Colton's knees buckled, and he clutched the Highlander for support. *Thank You, God.*

The officer finished his report and Colton descended the stairs to the street. He'd been right. The detectives wanted to look at his vehicle before he moved it. Which was fine with him. He didn't want to drive it until the damaged glass was replaced anyway.

After he slid into the passenger seat of the Silverado, Tanner made his way toward the four-lane. Little by little, the last remnants of fear and panic slowly dissipated, leaving room for annoyance, then anger.

He crossed his arms. "Jasmine had better have a really good reason for her phone being off."

He'd had a major scare and hadn't even been able to check on his son. That wasn't acceptable. As long as Jasmine was responsible for protecting Liam, he needed to be able to reach her.

Tanner shot him a sideways glance. "Maybe the battery went dead."

If that was the case, that wasn't acceptable, either. She needed to be able to call out in case of an emergency. Allowing her phone to go dead would be totally irresponsible.

When Tanner approached Colton's property, a Cherokee County cruiser was parked on the road, lights still flashing. The gate was closed, but Brutus wasn't in the front yard. Maybe Jasmine had brought him inside when the deputies arrived. But why were they still there, twenty minutes after radioing that Liam and Jasmine were safe?

Colton jumped from the Silverado. "Thanks for the ride."

When he swung open the gate, Tanner pulled inside. Colton wasn't surprised. Tanner wouldn't leave until he knew everything was all right. That was the kind of friend he'd been ever since the two of them had landed in the same group home at age thirteen.

The door swung open and Jasmine stepped onto the deck.

Colton stalked toward her. "Where is Liam?"

"Watching a movie."

"Why isn't your phone on?" His tone was several decibels louder than normal and filled with accusation.

Jasmine's brows drew together. "It *is* on. It's sitting on the kitchen counter, where I was cooking."

Cooking? He hadn't hired her to be cook or maid any more than he'd hired her to be babysitter. But that would be a conversation for later.

She frowned. "I was just getting ready to call you to ask why you sent cops to check on us. Is this all because you couldn't get ahold of me?"

"Someone left a note on my windshield at the courthouse this afternoon. That was before they shot at me."

Jasmine blanched. Her eyes swept over him, then bounced back up to his face. "Are you all right?"

"I wasn't hit. I'd dropped the note and bent to pick it up just as he fired."

The last of the color leached from her face. "If you hadn't bent over when you did…"

Tanner approached and stepped onto the deck with them. "Where are the officers?"

"They're checking the perimeter. When I filled them in on everything, they wanted to make sure no one was prowling around."

Tanner nodded. "I'll see if they found anything."

Jasmine watched him disappear around the side of the house, then opened the door to step back inside. A pleasant aroma drifted to him, along with a childish voice he instantly recognized—Liam was watching *Finding Dory*.

When Colton followed Jasmine into the living room, Brutus met them, tail wagging. The Christmas tree twinkled with hundreds of lights, and Liam was lying on the floor, a throw pillow he'd pulled from the couch beneath him. Colton closed the door, and Liam swiveled his head. "Daddy!"

Colton almost stumbled. He'd waited nearly six months to hear his name from his son's lips. Ignoring the dog, he scooped Liam up and held him close, heart swelling as a lump formed in his throat.

His eyes met Jasmine's. The joy filling his chest was reflected on her face. When the assignment was over, and he and Liam were safe again, how was he going to be able to let her go? What was her leaving going to do to Liam?

He placed his son back on the floor and straightened. "What happened with your phone?"

"I don't know, but I guarantee you it's on."

She marched into the kitchen and Colton followed. Two covered pots sat on the stove, but the burners under them were off. One held spaghetti sauce, based on the pleasant aroma that had wrapped around him the moment she opened the door.

Jasmine snatched her phone from the counter, swiped the screen and turned it to face him. "See, no missed calls."

He squinted. "And one bar." Cell service wasn't always reliable in the mountains. He'd have thought of that if he hadn't been so panicked. "We need to either get you a different provider or I need to program the landline number into my phone." He'd had it installed last week, for the sole purpose of monitoring the alarm.

She nodded. "If you ever can't reach me, call the landline. I'll answer it." She leaned back against the counter. "The note on your windshield, what did it say?"

"'You can run, but you can't hide.' Not very original, but he got his point across."

Determination entered her gaze. "I don't want you leaving the house without protection."

He closed his eyes, nausea churning in his gut. Jasmine was right. He and Liam were no longer safe here. But he had nowhere else to go. They'd be just as vulnerable at his home in Atlanta as they were in Murphy. Heading back to his in-laws' place in Montana wasn't an option. He wouldn't put them in danger. He wasn't licensed to practice there, anyway, and he couldn't afford to take any more time off.

"I have to work."

"Then it's time to call in more help. We need someone on you and someone on your son twenty-four-seven."

She was right. His son was his first priority. But if something happened to *him*, where would Liam be? Cade was far too irresponsible to raise a child. But Colton couldn't afford any more security. At least not the paid kind.

"Let me talk to Tanner and Bryce. I know they'll be glad to help out however they can." Neither Murphy nor Cherokee County had the manpower to provide twenty-four-hour protection. But one or both agencies would probably make regular patrols through the area. And Tanner and Bryce would drive by even more frequently, both on and off duty.

A knock sounded on the door. When Colton opened

it, one of the deputies stood on the deck, Tanner next to him. His partner was walking toward the car.

"We checked all the way around. No one was there. There aren't any signs that anyone has been snooping around here recently, either. But Tanner told us about what happened in town today, so we're going to try to make regular passes."

Colton thanked him, and he walked away to join his partner. Tanner held up a hand in farewell. "Since everything's good here, I'm going to go back to Ingles and pick up where I left off." He dropped his hand and let it rest on Colton's shoulder. "I'll be circling up Hilltop every time I pass by, but if you need me, just call. I don't care if it's the middle of the night."

"Thanks." Without even asking, Colton knew Bryce would say the same thing. When he'd moved to Murphy at age fifteen, Bryce had been his first friend.

After Tanner left, Colton closed the gate and let Brutus back outside. When he joined Jasmine in the kitchen, one burner was on High, the other on Medium.

"As good as this smells, I'm hesitant to have this conversation, but I only hired you to be our bodyguard."

"No offense, but if I have to eat takeout once more, I'm going to scream."

Colton winced. He'd never been a great cook. Though he'd done some cooking for Liam before and after the trip to Montana, he'd tried to take pity on Jasmine.

She removed the lid from a pot and peeked inside. It was two-thirds full of water, a thin layer of oil pooled on the surface. Tiny bubbles collected at the bottom.

She put the lid back on, then stirred the contents of the other pot. Just as he'd guessed, spaghetti sauce.

"By the way, you owe me $42.67."

He lifted a brow. "For what?"

"Groceries."

Tension spiked through him. "You took Liam to the grocery store?"

"I took him to the park last Friday, too. And we took him to the art walk and to church and a number of other places. And I've taken him to day care every weekday for the past two weeks."

He released a pent-up breath. She was right. Leaving the house had become dangerous only an hour ago.

The water finally came to a boil, and she stirred in half a bag of pasta. When it had resumed boiling, she turned the burner down and faced him.

"Why warn you?"

"What?"

"The note. If someone really intended to kill you this afternoon, why put the note on your windshield?"

She had a point. "Do you think the shooter missed me on purpose?"

"I don't know. It just doesn't fit. Who warns their victims before attacking?"

Colton sank into one of the kitchen chairs, dread settling over him.

Perez.

That was his MO. He toyed with all of his victims—stalking and terrorizing them. The games sometimes went on for weeks. But they always ended the same.

Perez was locked up. For life. No chance of parole.

But it didn't matter. He had thugs to do his bidding—two brothers, according to what Jasmine had learned. He'd see to it that they followed his pattern, so there'd be no doubt about who was behind every attack.

Colton had fought with every bit of legal expertise he had to secure a death sentence for Perez.

Instead, he'd secured his own.

He was on Perez's hit list.

And no one made it off alive.

Jasmine stalked from the kitchen into the living room, heading toward the front door. She'd already been outside a half dozen times to circle the yard, scan the woods and look up and down the road. Each time she'd seen nothing but a rural mountain neighborhood—safe, quiet and still.

Even though it was Sunday, they hadn't left the house. The past two weekends, Colton had insisted on taking Liam to church. Which meant she'd had to go, too. So she'd alternated between watching from the back of the sanctuary and patrolling outside the building.

This afternoon, Colton was viewing the service online. And she was doing almost as well avoiding it as she'd done the past two weeks.

Nothing against MountainView Community Church in particular. The people were friendly, the music inspiring and the pastor's message engaging. But she didn't do church. For good reason.

While she'd stood in the back listening to the band play and the attendees sing, something had tugged at her. She'd looked away several times, but the song lyrics projected on the screen up front kept drawing her gaze back.

Too many spoke of an intimate God, a God who so wanted a personal relationship with His creation that He sent His son to earth in the form of a baby.

The Christmas story had never bothered her before. Of course, she'd never taken the time to fully analyze its meaning. Now that she was doing that, she found the whole idea disconcerting. If she wasn't careful, the messages of those songs and the pastor's words were going to upend her long-held beliefs.

On her way to the front door, she cast a glance at

Colton. He sat on the couch with Liam nestled against his side clutching his little rabbit. If it wasn't so close to nap time, Liam probably wouldn't be so content.

Colton tilted his head toward the empty spot next to him. "You can join us if you'd like."

"Thanks. But I'm going to check things outside again." She probably wouldn't see anything different from what she'd seen the first six times.

Colton had talked to her about his enemy Friday night. For the next days and weeks, the two of them were going to be continually on edge, waiting for Perez's next move. Meanwhile, all they could do was wait.

After a peek out the front window, she opened the door and slipped outside. For the indeterminable future, she was going to be stuck at the house. Colton was even pulling Liam out of day care.

Jasmine glanced around the yard, then headed down the steps. Brutus plodded toward her. He'd made her a little nervous when she'd first met him, just because of his sheer size. The way he'd lowered his ears and eyed her warily hadn't helped, either.

After that initial greeting, he'd moved her from the *foe* to the *friend* category. Or more likely, *unknown* to *friend*.

When Brutus reached her, she sat on the top step, which put her face even with his. She scratched his cheeks and neck, and his tail wagged.

"You like that?"

In response, the tail wagged harder. She sometimes felt sorry for him, roaming the yard alone. But that was the reason Colton had gotten him—for protection, not as a house pet.

Brutus bounded off, then returned to lay a partially chewed tennis ball at her feet. She picked it up, hoping the moisture was left over from this morning's rain rather than dog slobber. When she tossed the ball, Brutus took off after it, catching it in midair.

Her phone buzzed in her back pocket, notification of an incoming text. She smiled at the name on the screen. Dom was more than a coworker. He was a friend. She had a good relationship with all Burch Security bodyguards, but she'd always felt closest to Dom. He was the big brother she'd never had.

His text was short—Good time to call?

She texted back a yes.

Moments later her ringtone sounded. As soon as she answered, Dom's voice came through the phone, tough but with an edge of playfulness.

"How's the second-best security guard in all of America?"

She grinned. She was second best because he'd claimed the number one slot a long time ago. "Fine." She picked up Brutus's ball and tossed it again. "Enjoying the clean mountain air. This assignment is getting me out of the city."

"Good for you. I just finished mine. Boyfriend-turned-blackmailer. The client decided she was tired of paying out. I caught the creep trying to climb in her second-story bedroom window. He got a little surprise."

Jasmine's lips lifted in a wry smile. That surprise probably came in the form of Dom's fist. He'd always been protective of women, sometimes in an extreme, obsessive way. He'd almost gotten himself in trouble a few times.

Except for a six-year stint with the Marines, until moving to Atlanta, he'd lived in Massachusetts. Or "Mass," as he called it. The heavy New England accent just added to his tough-guy persona. He was one of only two men on the planet that she'd trust with her life. The other was Gunn.

"Don't know what's next. How's yours going?"

"Not sure. The guy's a district attorney, has made some enemies. One of them is going after him and his son."

"No wife in the picture?"

"No wife." Just a handsome, heartbroken father and a little boy who was touching her heart in a way no one else ever had. Oh, to have an assignment like Dom just finished—uncomplicated and unemotional.

She picked up the ball again. Brutus wasn't showing any signs of winding down. As he took off after it, a Silverado pickup drew to a stop outside the fence. This time Tanner's wife, Paige, was with him. Jasmine had met them both at church her first Sunday there, along with several of Colton's other friends.

She disconnected the call with Dom, then opened the gate and motioned them inside. When they'd parked, she closed the gate behind them.

While his wife exited the passenger's side, Tanner climbed out from behind the wheel. "We went out to eat at ShoeBootie's with Andi and Bryce. Figured we'd stop by here and check in with you guys on our way home."

Jasmine led them toward the house. "Colton will be glad to see you."

Tanner stepped onto the deck behind her. "Any more threats?"

"No. But it's only been two days."

When she swung open the door, Colton shut off the TV. "I thought I heard voices outside."

Soon Tanner was positioned on the love seat with his arm around his wife, and Jasmine had taken a seat beside Colton.

Tanner crossed an ankle over the opposite knee. "I don't suppose there've been any new developments in the case."

Colton shook his head. "Not yet."

Liam climbed over his father to get into Jasmine's lap. She wrapped him in her arms and gave him a tight squeeze. When she glanced at Colton, conflicting emotions tumbled across his face. The concern she understood. When it came to his son, there was plenty to be concerned about.

She *didn't* understand the warmth. Or maybe she did and didn't want to acknowledge it. Somehow, it made her want to put distance between them, yet draw closer at the same time.

But accusation? As if she'd intentionally wormed her way into his son's heart?

She gritted her teeth. He'd said he didn't want his son getting attached to her. But she'd only been doing her job. Well, maybe comforting him during his nightmares fell a little outside of those job responsibilities.

But how could she deny him what she'd longed for at his age when it was within her power to give?

He slid from her lap and ran toward the kitchen. When he disappeared into his room, Colton crossed his arms, his gaze shifting to his friend. "The authorities in Atlanta have been working to identify the men responsible for the break-in and attempted kidnapping. I've had several conversations with them. My former administrative assistant has, too. We've given them the names of everyone we can think of who might want to exact some vengeance. They're also looking at recently released inmates, seeing if I was involved in any of their cases."

Tanner nodded. "From what I hear, Cherokee County is throwing in some of their resources now, too."

"Good," Colton said. "Since that note, Atlanta PD is putting special focus on one defendant in particular. We wrapped up his case the week before Mandy died. At that time, he made some pretty serious threats."

"That was seven months ago. Why wait till now to act?"

"Four weeks after he made his threats, I left for Montana. Then I was back home only a week before coming up here."

Tanner pursed his lips. "The reference to you running."

"My thoughts exactly. Ransacking my house, trying to take my son, leaving threatening notes that let me know he's watching—that's his style. He stalks his victims, making them almost crazy with fear before he finally takes them out."

Liam returned to the room holding his stuffed rabbit. This time he made a beeline for Paige, whose face lit with a broad smile. She obviously loved kids. The boy lifted his arms, the rabbit dangling from one hand, and she dragged him onto her lap. When he snuggled against her chest, she rocked him back and forth.

Colton nodded toward his son. "I'm pulling him out of day care. I think it'll be easier for Jasmine to protect him if he stays here in the house. But I have to hire a babysitter. Jasmine needs to be free to patrol without distractions."

He rose and began to pace. "After my last babysitter ended up bound and gagged in the closet, I'm a little hesitant. I still haven't come up with a solution."

Paige wrapped her hand around one of Liam's. "I can do it. At least until the next term starts."

Tanner stared her down, a tic in his jaw. "Colton knows I'd do almost anything for him, but putting my wife in danger is where I draw the line."

Paige shifted her position to face him more fully. "It sounds like the creep is still in the stalking stage."

"He tried to kidnap Liam." Exasperation filled Tanner's tone.

"Now Liam has a bodyguard. And in case you've forgotten, I can pretty well hold my own."

"Two wom—" Tanner cut himself off midphrase, apparently second-guessing the opinion he was about to express.

Paige sighed. "Look, it's only during the day, while Colton is at work. Won't you guys and Cherokee County be doing some drive-bys anyway?"

"Occasionally." Tanner still didn't look happy. "What about in between times?"

"There are still two lines of defense—Brutus and Jasmine."

"What if someone shoots her?"

Jasmine lifted her brows.

"Sorry, but it's a possibility."

"I'll be wearing Kevlar."

She was stating a fact, not taking sides. She wasn't sure whose side to take in the argument. She tended to agree with Paige, that Perez, or whoever, was still in the stalking stage.

Colton was right about needing to hire a babysitter. She couldn't effectively do her job if all her attention was on watching Liam. Paige was as good a choice as anyone. Probably better. Jasmine didn't know anything about her background, but that statement about being able to hold her own was encouraging.

When Tanner and Paige left a short time later, Liam climbed back onto Jasmine's lap. Colton patted his son's back.

"Okay, buddy, it's nap time."

Liam wrapped his little arms around her waist and squeezed. "No."

"How about if Miss Jasmine puts you to bed?"

He was silent for several moments, as if thinking about his answer. "'Kay."

Colton helped her to her feet, Liam still wrapped around her. After laying him on his side in his bed, she positioned the rabbit in his arms, then rubbed his back for several moments. "Sleep good."

His thumb slipped into his mouth, and she straightened. Colton stood leaning against the chest of drawers next to the door, arms crossed. His posture said *restrained*, maybe even a little defensive.

But that was not what his eyes said. His gaze was warm, filled with admiration. Something else, too. As if he was looking at her, not simply as his son's protector. But as a woman.

She swallowed hard. She was seeing what she wanted to see. She'd found Colton attractive right from the start. Cade, too, since their looks were identical. But Colton's depth and seriousness appealed to her far more than Cade's flippancy.

Her eyes shifted to the framed portrait sitting atop the dresser. The perfect happy family—successful husband and father, beautiful wife and mother, sweet child, the product of their love.

She didn't belong in that picture. Even with Mandy gone, that empty slot was one she could never hope to fill.

She strode toward the door. When her gaze met Colton's, whatever she thought she'd seen was gone.

"I'm going outside." This time she'd stay out for a while, throwing the ball for Brutus, circling the yard however many times she had to. Whatever it took, she'd crush the feelings Colton stirred in her and end this longing for something she could never have.

She stepped onto the deck, again envious of Dom's easy assignment. But no matter how difficult this one was turning out to be on a personal level, something told her she was exactly what Liam needed at this point in his life.

As far as Liam's handsome father, she didn't know what he needed.

But she was pretty sure she didn't have it.

SIX

A terrified scream pierced the quiet.

Colton clawed his way to consciousness. The shriek that had jarred him awake wasn't the first. There'd been at least one other. It hovered in the back of his mind, like the remnant of a dream.

He sprang from the bed and darted into the living room. Why hadn't he come instantly awake? He certainly wasn't letting down his guard.

Or maybe he was, on a subconscious level. Maybe after six months of middle-of-the-night screams, having someone else to ease the burden was working its way into his psyche. Knowing Jasmine never let down her guard, he was slowly letting down his, at least in sleep.

When he shot through Liam's open door, Jasmine was sitting in the rocking chair, already holding him. Brutus lay nearby. Yesterday morning's rain had ushered in a cold front. With temperatures expected to dip near freezing, Colton hadn't had the heart to leave him outside.

He knelt in front of the chair to cup his son's head. Except for some quiet whimpers, he was still. "You okay, buddy?"

Liam drew in a shuddering breath through his nose,

not willing to give up the security of his thumb. His free arm was stretched along Jasmine's side.

When Colton had first met her, he'd pegged her as not the motherly type. He'd obviously been wrong.

He glanced behind him to check the digital clock on the dresser—5:12. His own alarm would be going off in another forty-five minutes. It wouldn't be worth trying to go back to sleep. "Sorry about the short night."

"No problem. I was awake anyway." Her voice was a soft murmur.

He matched her tone. Liam seemed to be going back to sleep. "You've said that before."

"I sleep in bursts. I've never required a lot."

Maybe she didn't, but she probably needed more than she got. She'd likely just conditioned her body to function well in a continuously sleep-deprived state.

"You should try to work in another burst before daylight."

She gave him a half smile. "I might do that."

He'd get ready for work, have his quiet time, then whip up some breakfast. He wasn't a great cook, but he made some mean scrambled eggs. And he could usually manage toast without burning it.

He leaned back to sit on the floor, giving his knees a break. "I appreciate what you're doing for him. You're really good with him."

"I don't mind. He's an easy kid to love." She closed her eyes and placed a soft kiss on the top of his head.

Colton's heart swelled. Watching Jasmine play a motherly role, treating Liam with such tenderness, did funny things to his insides. He was still having a hard time reconciling the tough ex-MP who put him on the floor in Gunter Burch's office with the gentle woman whose presence was bringing such healing to his son.

God had brought her into their lives. When Colton had walked into Burch Security, he'd known what he wanted—a burly monster of a guy no one would mess with. Instead, God gave him five-foot-two-inch Jasmine, tough as nails but with an unexpected gentleness, sympathetic with their struggles because she'd had plenty of her own.

When Jasmine opened her eyes, her gaze locked with his and held. Something he couldn't put a name to passed between them. He'd seen it yesterday, too, when they'd put Liam down for his nap—a hint that she might need them as much as they needed her. Then she'd looked away, walked from the room and escaped outside.

She continued her gentle rocking motion. "You're an amazing father. I know it's got to be tough."

He nodded. He wouldn't try to downplay what he'd been through. Trying to keep his son from retreating completely while drowning in his own grief. Struggling to be both father and mother and feeling he was failing miserably at both.

Since she'd come, some of that overwhelming burden had lifted. Now her expressive brown eyes tugged at him. Encouragement and respect swam in their depths, along with the same sense of longing he'd briefly witnessed during those rare unguarded moments.

"I sense that you've been through your own traumas. I can see it in your eyes."

She shrugged, her eyes shifting sideways. "Everyone has their burdens to bear."

"And some burdens are especially heavy."

She pulled her lower lip between her teeth. For several moments, the only sound was the gentle creak of the rocking chair. When she finally spoke, she didn't look at him. "His name was Zach, one of the few guys I ever loved."

Silence stretched between them again. "We were stationed together in Afghanistan. It was early in the morning. Everyone was getting ready to start their day. Someone shouted 'Incoming.' Then total chaos. Zach was hit. He died in my arms."

Colton rested a hand on her knee. "I'm sorry."

She shrugged again. "I think Liam's asleep."

Colton wasn't surprised at the abrupt subject change. "I'll put him back in bed."

When he tried to lift Liam from her lap, the boy pulled his thumb from his mouth. That arm joined the other to partially circle Jasmine's body, and he tightened his hold.

"Mommy."

The single word was barely audible. But it left Colton with the sensation that someone had thrown a bucket of ice water in his face.

Jasmine's reaction was the same. Her lips parted, and her brows drew together. He might have even seen panic flash in her eyes.

Colton turned away, trying to rein in his emotions. Maybe Liam was remembering his mother, pretending that was who held him. Or maybe he'd already made the substitution in his mind. If the latter, memories of Mandy would quickly fade. Maybe they would anyway.

His gaze locked on the framed eight-by-ten photograph atop the dresser. It sat in shadow, barely touched by the soft glow of the night-light.

But he didn't need light to see the picture clearly in his mind. It had been taken at Christmastime a year ago, the last professional one they'd had done. Mandy was hugging a laughing Liam, her eyes shining with love and joy.

She'd loved their son more than life itself. Colton

couldn't let Liam forget her. He had to help him hang on to her memory as long as possible. He just didn't know how.

There was rustling behind him as Jasmine rose and a soft creak when she placed Liam in his bed.

Colton swallowed hard and spoke without turning around. "I'll wake you up well before I have to leave."

Even as he spoke the words, he knew he wouldn't have to. No matter how rough the night, Jasmine never slept past sunup.

He left the room and returned to his own. He was having to rely on Bryce for a ride to work. But tonight he'd have his vehicle back. Curtis Home & Auto Glass had the windshield and window replacements scheduled for today.

After dressing, he slipped his wallet and keys into his pocket, then picked up his phone. Sometime during the night, two texts had come through. He touched the icon. Both were from the same unknown number.

His chest tightened. Who would text him in the middle of the night from an unknown number?

He touched the screen again to bring up the messages. The first was short—Sleeping well? The simple question held a sinister undertone.

The second text was an all-out threat—Instead you should be watching your back.

He struggled in a constricted breath, the sense of being watched so powerful it almost paralyzed him. He'd had the same personal cell number for years. It was private, known only to friends and family.

But Perez had a long reach, with control over people in high places. And he used those connections to strike terror into the hearts of his victims.

Colton spurred his legs to action, his phone still

gripped in one white-knuckled fist. He needed to wake up Jasmine so she could be alert and armed. Or maybe they should all get in the Highlander and run.

Outside Liam's room, he skidded to a stop. He needed to get a grip. He knew Perez well enough to know how he worked. When he was ready to strike, it would be without warning.

When Brutus plodded into the kitchen, Colton led him to the front and disarmed the alarm. After letting the dog out, he started the coffeepot. He'd nurse his two cups while enjoying his morning prayer and Bible reading. Then he'd make breakfast.

Paige would be arriving around the time he'd have to leave. The thought sent conflicting emotions tumbling through him—guilt over allowing his friend to put herself in possible danger, and relief that she'd be here backing up Jasmine.

Paige was right. She could hold her own. He hadn't seen her in action, but he'd heard enough stories to know she wasn't bluffing.

He added some flavored creamer to his coffee and headed into the living room. Before moving to his favorite chair, he stepped on the floor switch at the other end of the room, and the lights blanketing the Christmas tree's branches woke up. He didn't know about Jasmine, but Liam was enjoying the tree. Colton was, too. The decorations lent warmth and cheer to the house, qualities that were augmented by Jasmine's presence.

He settled into his chair and clicked on the floor lamp. His Kindle sat on the end table next to him, but his Bible reading would wait a few minutes.

Tipping back his head and closing his eyes, he thanked God that Paige would soon be on her way over.

And he thanked God for sending Jasmine.

Both to protect him and his son and to help them heal.

And since God had sent her, he asked Him to also help them pick up the pieces when it was time for her to leave.

Pleasant aromas drifted into the room, and Jasmine opened her eyes. Light seeped in around the Captain America curtains, too bright to be the first glimpse of daybreak.

She bolted upright with a gasp, searching out the clock. It was just past 7:30. Liam was still asleep, curled on his side with one thumb in his mouth, his other arm wrapped around his little rabbit. The bedroom door was closed. Colton must have shut it so he wouldn't disturb her.

After gathering a change of clothes, along with her vest and holster, she eased the door open. The scent of breakfast hit her full force. Colton stood in front of the stove, pushing scrambled eggs around a skillet with a wooden spoon. Contents of another pot simmered on the small back burner. Several pieces of fried bacon sat on a paper-towel-lined plate.

Jasmine leaned against the doorjamb, not ready to announce her presence. She was used to the professional Colton, dressed in a suit, heading out to continue his fight for justice. And she'd seen him in the role of father numerous times.

But watching the domestic Colton move about the kitchen preparing breakfast for her and his son warmed her inside. The problem with that warmth was how longing always followed, the desire for things that were out of her reach. At least with the man in front of her.

"Brutus is outside?"

Colton turned, brows lifted in surprise. "I let him out as soon as I got up."

"I'm getting dressed, then taking a look around before breakfast."

"Be careful." He laid down the spoon and pulled his phone from his pocket.

She hesitated. There was a stiffness to his movements. "Is everything okay?"

Instead of answering, he touched the screen a couple times and handed her the phone.

She skimmed the words, her tension increasing with each one. "You should have woken me up."

"I started to, then decided to let you get your rest." He returned to his breakfast preparations. "He's still playing with me. If this is Perez, that's how he works. He's an expert in fear and manipulation."

"It's disconcerting he has your cell number."

Leaving Colton in the kitchen, she headed toward the bathroom off the side of the living room. It was a full bath rather than a partial, but instead of a tub/shower combo, it had one of those small walk-in shower units. But it was her own space. Much more comfortable than sharing the larger master bath with Colton.

Two minutes later, she emerged dressed in jeans, boots and a sweater, her bulletproof vest hidden beneath and her holster affixed to her belt. She crossed the living room and looked out one of the front windows. From her vantage point, no one was there. All was still under a gloomy, gray sky. Brutus was apparently around one of the sides or in the back. As she watched, a gust swept through, blowing dead leaves across the yard.

She lifted her heavy coat from the hook by the door, slipped into it and walked outside, locking the door behind her. After scanning her surroundings, she moved down the steps. Before she reached the bottom, Brutus appeared at the corner of the house, body rigid with tension. He immediately relaxed and bounded up to her.

She bent to pet him. She wasn't letting down her guard, but if anyone was out there, Brutus would have let her know. He seemed to share her constant state of alertness. She straightened. Her rounds would be abbreviated this morning, since Colton would be ready for breakfast once he'd gotten Liam up.

She released a sigh. She'd told Colton that Liam was an easy kid to love. That was exactly what had happened. She'd fallen in love with the sad little boy.

But she was trying hard to keep her distance from Liam's handsome, hurting father, no matter how much her heart wanted to do otherwise. Colton and Liam needed stability, something she would never be able to provide.

Her own history proved it. From her mom's string of boyfriends who screamed curses and slapped her around to her own failed relationships, anything more than friendship never turned out well. Even her latest. Although she'd loved Zach, she'd had to admit that her relationship with him wasn't much less dysfunctional than the others.

Colton deserved better. Someday, someone as amazing as Mandy would walk into his life. When that happened, she hoped he'd be ready. For both his sake and Liam's.

She moved toward the side, gaze scanning the mix of evergreens and mostly bare hardwoods that made up the scenery there. As she did her rounds, Brutus walked beside her.

This assignment was turning out to be a mistake, all the way around. Colton had feared that his little boy would get attached to her. He'd done what he could to make sure that didn't happen, enrolling him in day care and taking care of Liam himself evenings and weekends.

Unfortunately, it hadn't worked. And early this morning, Liam had called her Mommy. Instead of finding the name endearing, she'd felt like she'd been punched in the gut. Colton had turned away, but not before she'd seen the hurt on his face.

During her time in the Gale household, she'd watched Liam take small steps and slowly reengage with his surroundings. In trying to help the little boy heal, she'd thought she was doing a good thing.

Now she knew better. In the end, her involvement would do more harm than good.

Over the past two and a half weeks, Liam had already started viewing her as a mother figure. No matter what she and Colton did, he was only going to get more attached. When the assignment ended, he'd find his little world shattered for a second time.

She followed the back fence, Brutus still walking next to her. Breakfast could wait a few more minutes. She needed to call Gunn. Dom was finished with his assignment. Although he wasn't ideal for this one, he was a better choice than she was.

Jasmine sighed. She'd never given up on a job, no matter how difficult. She wasn't a quitter. But this was different. She'd been fighting her attraction toward Colton almost from the moment she'd met him. And she was losing the battle.

But it was more than that. A child's emotional health was at stake.

She glanced at the house. Colton had opened the curtains over the sink and now stood framed in the window, watching her. He lifted a hand, and she waved back. Her heart squeezed.

When she turned the corner to head toward the front, she pulled her phone from her pocket and brought up Gunn's cell number. He answered on the second ring.

She skipped the pleasantries. "I'm the wrong person for this job. You need to put Dom on it."

"Two and a half weeks ago, you showed Mr. Gale you were the *right* person for the job. Did something change?"

"It's not Colt—Mr. Gale. It's his son."

"You're letting a three-year-old run you off?" Gunn's tone held barely restrained humor.

She heaved an exasperated sigh. "It's not like that at all. Liam is precious."

"And what about his father?"

"He's…fine." Several other adjectives flitted through her mind, but she wasn't about to pass any of those along to Gunn. If her former commander had any inkling of the feelings she was developing for her client, she'd never hear the end of it.

Gunn was only twelve years her senior, but too often, he tried to slip into a father role. He'd been there when Zach was killed and over the following months had helped her come to grips with it. She owed him a lot.

But as well as he knew her, sometimes he was totally off base. Just because he'd been happily married for most of his adult life didn't mean she was cut out for a stable relationship.

She pulled her thoughts from Colton and focused on his son. "Less than seven months ago, Liam lost his mother. Now he's getting attached to me." She paused, closing her eyes. "He called me Mommy."

"You're worried that the boy is getting attached to you, but it sounds like that's already happened. What does his father think?"

"He hasn't said."

"And he hasn't spoken with me, either. If he's worried about it, he'll give me a call. Until then, I think you might be exactly where you need to be."

She tightened her hand around the phone. Gunn was probably thinking he'd found her a ready-made family. Another example of him believing he knew what was best for her when he had no clue.

"You're not old enough to be my father, so stop trying to act like one."

The clipped tone obviously didn't annoy her boss. Instead of a reprimand, she got good-natured laughter. She reached the end of the front fence and headed toward the house. Beside her, Brutus stiffened, then shot away.

"Gotta run." She ended the call with Gunn and hurried after the dog, weapon drawn.

Brutus had stopped at the back fence and stood staring into the woods. The hair on his back was raised, and a low growl rumbled in his chest.

"What is it, boy? Do you see something?"

She scanned the woods, but whatever he'd seen was gone.

Finally, Brutus relaxed. Jasmine had just started to walk away when a loud rustle sounded nearby. She spun, swinging her weapon around. Two squirrels chased each other along the outside of the fence and up a nearby pine.

She released a nervous laugh, scratching the back of Brutus's neck. "We're going into fight mode over a couple of squirrels."

She shook her head and walked toward the house. When she entered the kitchen, Colton already had Liam dressed and in his high chair and was dishing up their plates. He turned and gave her a half smile that was in direct conflict with the worry in his eyes. "Everything okay out there?"

"Yeah. Brutus's meltdown was nothing more than a couple of squirrels playing."

After an especially somber breakfast, Colton disappeared into the master bedroom, then returned ready for work, blond hair combed into soft layers. He'd already been wearing his suit pants and long-sleeved dress shirt. Now a jacket and tie completed the ensemble.

Her heart stuttered. It wasn't just his good looks. It was the whole scenario—the man of the house heading off to work to provide a stable home for his family.

He approached the table, then bent over the high chair to hug and kiss his son. Suddenly she wanted one, too—a hug or a kiss. Or both.

Instead, she got a wave and a caution to be careful.

A horn tooted outside and Colton crossed the living room to peer out the front window. "Bryce is here. Paige should be arriving any minute, but I'm still going to close the gate behind me."

"Sounds good. She'll let herself in."

Jasmine spooned the last of the grits into her mouth. When Liam finished, she took him down from the high chair and wiped his hands. Sudden barking set her nerves on edge. Her hand stilled, Liam's fingers still wrapped inside the washcloth. She straightened, every sense on alert.

Brutus wasn't letting her know Paige had arrived. Paige would be stopping at the front gate. Brutus was in the back. Maybe what he'd seen before had been a real threat and not simply squirrels.

She moved to the kitchen sink and peered past the edge of the curtain, which Colton had closed. Brutus stood at the back fence staring into the woods. His head and body jerked in time with the barks. He fell silent for several seconds, then resumed the ferocious barking. Judging from his stiff stance, and the way the fur stood up on the back of his neck, the periods between rounds of barking were probably filled with deep-throated growls.

From her vantage point, she couldn't see anything suspicious. Other than a highly agitated dog. And she couldn't go out to investigate. Not with Liam inside the house alone.

Letting the curtains fall, she moved into the living room. She'd heard Colton lock the dead bolt with his key but couldn't ignore the compulsion to double-check. When that was done, she headed back to the kitchen, then into Liam's room. His window offered the same view as the kitchen one, just a slightly different angle. Whatever Brutus was barking at, she couldn't see it from inside the house.

Where was Paige? She was supposed to arrive close to the time Colton left. Of course, it *was* close to the time Colton left. He hadn't been gone more than five minutes.

When she turned from the window, Liam was standing in the doorway.

"Legos?" His voice sounded so sweet. Knowing his history, every word he spoke warmed her heart.

"Sure, sweetie. You can play with your Legos."

He picked up the plastic bin and poured its contents onto the bedroom floor. She didn't know what he planned to make, and she wasn't going to stay there long enough to find out.

"I'm going to see if Miss Paige is here yet. Call me if you need me, okay?"

Liam didn't look up from his activities. "Okay."

She stepped back into the kitchen. Brutus was still barking. It didn't sound like he'd changed positions, either. The barking was reassuring. If someone came into the yard, he'd just attack. So whoever had him in such an uproar was still outside the fence. And he apparently didn't have a tranquilizer dart.

She moved into the living room and peered out one of the front windows. The gate was ajar. Colton would have closed it. And Paige would open it fully so she could park her vehicle in the driveway. Instead, it was open about two feet—just enough for someone to slip through.

Was the commotion in the back a decoy, a way to draw Brutus to the rear fence while someone accessed the house from the front?

Jasmine reset the alarm and put her hand on her weapon. She hadn't drawn it yet, because she hadn't wanted to startle Liam. But she was alert and ready.

She scanned the yard, looking for signs of movement. There were plenty of hiding places. Like behind that huge hemlock. But intruders wouldn't be able to get to the front door without her seeing them. If they broke a window, she'd hear the glass shatter.

She leaned closer to the windowpane. Paige suddenly shot out from behind the hemlock and sprinted the few yards to the driveway. She ran around the Suburban and disappeared from view.

Jasmine disarmed the alarm, then swung open the door and stepped onto the deck, weapon drawn. A man sprang to his feet on the other side of the SUV. A ski mask hid his face, but the eyes peering through the holes were wide.

A second later, Paige was on him, fists swinging. Though the guy tried to block her punches, several found their mark.

Jasmine raised her weapon. "Hands in the air, or I'll shoot."

The intruder spun and ran toward the fence. Three

steps later, Paige tackled him, and they both disappeared from view, the vehicle blocking them.

Jasmine hesitated. The man Paige had tackled wasn't the only threat. Someone else was in back. Maybe they intended to lure her away from the house so Liam would be unprotected.

It wasn't going to work. As concerned as she was for Paige's safety, she wasn't going to abandon her responsibility to Colton's little boy.

Several seconds passed before she realized that Brutus had stopped barking. Except for some thumps and grunts from the other side of the vehicle, the morning was eerily quiet.

When the man rose, his mask was cockeyed. But Jasmine didn't get a good look at him. He again made a beeline for the fence.

Paige charged off after him, and Brutus resumed barking, louder and closer. He appeared around the side of the house as the man slung himself over the top rail of the fence. Paige grabbed his leg, but he slipped through her grasp and disappeared into the woods. When she made her way around the Suburban, she was limping.

Jasmine frowned. "You're hurt." It was amazing she wasn't dead. Whatever had possessed her to attack someone half again her size?

"I'm all right." She motioned toward the road. "I need to bring my car into the yard."

Jasmine glanced that direction, but the hemlock blocked the view of whatever she'd driven.

Paige continued. "As I was coming up on Colton's place, the creep was walking along the other side of your car. Then he squatted down. I pulled off the road, slipped through the gate and tackled him." She frowned. "I think

I got to him before he had a chance to do anything, but I'm going to look at your brake lines to be sure."

"You're a mechanic, too?" Nothing would surprise her at this point.

She shrugged. "I've picked up bits and pieces over the years, enough to recognize if brakes have been tampered with."

Paige went to retrieve her vehicle, and Jasmine headed back inside to call 911 and check on Liam. She unclipped her phone from her belt, then picked up Colton's cordless instead. She'd had one bar. Her signal was better outside than inside.

While she waited for her 911 call to connect, she stood in Liam's doorway. He fished through the colorful pile on his floor and picked up a rectangular piece. "This one."

She smiled. He was even starting to talk to himself. A good sign, something she'd share with Colton when he got home.

Leaving Liam to his play, she moved to the front of the house. When she finished relaying everything to the 911 dispatcher, she stepped onto the deck. A Dodge Charger sat in the drive. Paige was limping toward the opposite side of the Suburban, favoring the injured leg. She disappeared, rose a half minute later, then disappeared again.

As she walked back around, she made a fist, thumb raised. "So far, so good."

She again lowered herself to the ground, gripping the front wheel well for support. Jasmine shook her head. Tanner wasn't going to be happy with either of them.

Once she'd checked the rear, she straightened. "Everything's fine."

Jasmine released a pent-up breath. If Paige hadn't come when she had...

The commotion in the back was definitely a decoy,

something to distract the dog and get Jasmine to focus her attention behind the house. She wouldn't fall for that ploy again.

Paige followed her inside and sank onto the couch.

Jasmine stared down at her, hands on her hips. "I don't know whether to scold you or thank you."

Paige shifted position and winced. "How about neither?"

"You'd probably rather I don't say anything to Tanner, too."

"Yeah, that would be good."

Jasmine sat on the opposite end of the couch. "I was going to ask you what your superpower was. I don't think that's necessary now."

"My superpower?"

"You reminded Tanner you could hold your own, so I knew there's more to you than meets the eye."

Paige gave a sharp nod. "Street fighting. Hand-to-hand combat."

"You good with a gun?"

She shrugged. "Not bad."

"Did you bring one?"

"Can't."

Jasmine cocked a brow, but Paige didn't explain.

"How long have you and Tanner been together?" She'd give Paige a reprieve for now. But that didn't mean she wouldn't circle back to the topic before the end of the day. If the woman was going to be around Colton and Liam, it was her job to know what secrets she harbored.

"Married eight months. Dated almost two years before that." Paige gave her a crooked smile. "Took me a while to give in and take the plunge."

Liam padded into the room, his stockinged feet almost silent against the hardwood floor. "Water, peez."

"Sure, sweetie." Her response came in unison with Paige's.

Paige held up a hand. "I'm the babysitter, remember?"

Jasmine nodded. "I'll be outside."

She'd make her rounds until the police arrived, then take over the babysitter role while Paige came out and talked to them.

After scanning the front yard through one of the windows, she opened the door and stepped onto the deck. For the next ten minutes, she walked the yard, studying the woods beyond the fence. The man who'd run from Paige had trampled down underbrush and kicked up leaves in his rush to escape. Whoever had had Brutus in an uproar hadn't left so obvious a trail.

Approaching sirens drew her eyes to the road. An emergency vehicle was making its way up Hilltop. She opened the gate and flagged in a Cherokee County sheriff cruiser.

The uniformed deputy stepped out and introduced himself. "You called about someone tampering with a vehicle?"

"I did." She relayed what little she'd witnessed. "But the lady you really need to speak with is inside."

She jogged to the house and sent Paige out. When she checked on Liam, he'd returned to his Legos. He looked up at her, and his mouth lifted in a smile. "Movie?"

"Which one do you want to see?"

"Cars."

Two minutes later, she'd located the DVD and had the credits rolling. As soon as she laid the remote on the coffee table, a small hand slipped into hers.

"You want me to watch it with you?"

He nodded. When she sank onto the couch, he climbed

up next to her. She put her arm around him, and he snuggled against her side.

She closed her eyes and dipped her head, breathing in his strawberry-scented shampoo. Her chest tightened in a combination of love and longing.

This was precisely the reason she'd tried so hard to get Gunn to reassign her. Whatever he was trying to do, it was likely to turn out poorly for both her and Liam.

When a soft knock sounded sometime later, she rose to let Paige in.

Paige locked the door behind her. "I closed and latched the gate."

"Good. I don't suppose the deputy found anything."

"No. He headed into the woods the same direction the guy had gone, then came back a few minutes later. Didn't see anything. The other one found where it looked like someone had tromped through the woods in the back, but didn't find anyone there, either."

Paige returned to her babysitting duties, and Jasmine stepped back outside. After spending the morning alternating between patrolling the yard and checking on things inside, she sat down to grilled ham-and-cheese sandwiches Paige had prepared.

"Thanks for lunch." She picked up her sandwich, still hot from the griddle. "So, what are we keeping you from? What do you normally do with your days?"

"I'm taking classes at the community college, but as of today, I'm on Christmas break."

"What are you studying?"

"My Gen Eds now, but next term I'll start education classes. I'm working toward getting my teaching certificate."

"I didn't think you could teach school if you were a felon."

"Who said I was a felon?"

"You did, but not in so many words."

Paige shrugged. "That was another lifetime."

"Considering you're married to a cop and are a regular church attender, I gathered as much."

Paige gave her a half smile. "Back to the teacher question, it depends on the felony. I never killed or molested anyone." The smile widened. "Although I was tempted to run that creep's head into the ground this morning." She sobered and a fierceness entered her eyes. "Thinking about anyone threatening Liam just about makes me lose it."

Jasmine nodded. She liked Paige. Tough and no-nonsense. She was a good one to have around.

She'd told Tanner she could hold her own.

After watching her this morning, Jasmine agreed wholeheartedly.

"FAST FIVE" READER SURVEY

Your participation entitles you to:
✳ 4 Thank-You Gifts Worth Over $20!

Complete the survey in minutes.

Get **2 FREE** Books

Your Thank-You Gifts include **2 FREE BOOKS** and **2 MYSTERY GIFTS**. There's no obligation to purchase anything!

See inside for details.

Dear Reader,

Since you are a lover of our books, your opinions are important to us... and so is your time.

That's why we made sure your **"FAST FIVE" READER SURVEY** can be completed in just a few minutes. Your answers to the five questions will help us remain at the forefront of women's fiction.

And, as a thank-you for participating, we'd like to send you **4 FREE THANK-YOU GIFTS!**

Enjoy your gifts with our appreciation,

Pam Powers

To get your
4 FREE THANK-YOU GIFTS:

✳ Quickly complete the "Fast Five" Reader Survey
and return the insert.

"FAST FIVE" READER SURVEY

1 Do you sometimes read a book a second or third time? ○ Yes ○ No

2 Do you often choose reading over other forms of entertainment such as television? ○ Yes ○ No

3 When you were a child, did someone regularly read aloud to you? ○ Yes ○ No

4 Do you sometimes take a book with you when you travel outside the home? ○ Yes ○ No

5 In addition to books, do you regularly read newspapers and magazines? ○ Yes ○ No

YES! I have completed the above Reader Survey. Please send me my 4 FREE GIFTS (gifts worth over $20 retail). I understand that I am under no obligation to buy anything, as explained on the back of this card.

❏ I prefer the regular-print edition
153/353 IDL GM3W

❏ I prefer the larger-print edition
107/307 IDL GM3W

FIRST NAME	LAST NAME

ADDRESS

APT.#	CITY

STATE/PROV.	ZIP/POSTAL CODE

SLI-817-FF18

SEVEN

Colton stepped from the courthouse under a steel-gray sky. The weather had been cold and dreary for the past two days.

But that wasn't the reason for his dark mood. When he'd gotten home yesterday evening, Jasmine had told him about the events of the morning. His enemies had been watching, waiting until he left and Jasmine was alone with Liam.

It all about drove him nuts—waiting for the next strike, unable to predict when or where it was going to happen.

He didn't do well with helplessness. It had been a constant companion through most of his childhood as he'd been shuffled from one foster home to the next. He'd thought that once he became an adult, he'd never feel helpless again.

But it wasn't a malady reserved for unwanted children. For the past six months, he'd suffered through more than his fair share, at a loss as to how to help his son and defenseless against the grief that threatened to drown them both.

Last night, he'd taken out his fear and frustration on Jasmine, demanding to know why she hadn't called him immediately. She'd stood her ground, and she'd been right. There'd been no reason to intrude into his work-day. No one was hurt, and there was nothing he could have done anyway.

He hurried through the parking lot, glancing around him. Next on the agenda was a trip to the grocery store, with Tanner accompanying him. According to Tanner's text, he was already there, probably inspecting the High-lander.

Colton had gotten it back yesterday afternoon. Now it was parked at the rear of the courthouse next to the parking for the senior center. The area was open, with no trees for someone to hide behind.

When Colton approached, Tanner was lying next to the SUV, looking beneath. After Jasmine and Paige's experience, they'd all agreed—no cranking vehicles without first checking them.

Tanner rose. "So far, so good."

As he circled around to the front, Colton's phone rang. He frowned. Cade was calling. Three days had passed since the last warning. Apparently, it was time for an-other one.

Colton put the phone to his ear and greeted his twin. Cade's "how are you?" seemed to hold more meaning than the three words usually did.

"We're all fine. How is your trip going?"

"Could be better. I've been looking for a particular piece. Everything similar seems to be locked away in someone's private collection."

"I'm sure you'll find what you're looking for." He al-ways did.

Colton was smart, but he'd always had to work for what he got. Cade was brilliant. Everything seemed to come easily to him, gift wrapped and delivered on a golden platter. He'd partied his way through college and still managed to maintain a 3.8 GPA.

And no one could deny that he was good at what he did. He had a knack for finding the deals and turning everything he touched to gold. Their adoptive father had always been able to make a nice profit, but Cade's success lately had been phenomenal.

Tanner finished his inspection and held up both thumbs.

Colton opened the driver door. "I've got to run. Tanner and I are getting ready to do some grocery shopping."

"You guys actually made plans to grocery shop together?" Cade released a throaty laugh. "That's as bad as some of the girls I've dated who won't go to the restroom without a friend."

Colton winced. "We're keeping Liam inside, and I'm trying to avoid going anywhere alone at night." In fact, if he hadn't had a midafternoon appointment across town, Tanner would have insisted on dropping him off in the morning and picking him up at the end of the day.

He stepped into the opening but didn't get in. "We've had some threats."

"What kind of threats?"

"Just random stuff." He didn't need to worry his brother. Colton almost laughed at the absurdity of the thought. Until two and a half weeks ago, it wouldn't have crossed his mind. He'd never seen Cade worry about anything.

"You've got to get Liam out of there." Cade spoke with urgency bordering on panic.

Colton sighed. So much for not worrying his brother. "I don't have anywhere to go. Even if those guys have found us, it's different now. Liam doesn't have a baby-sitter. He has a bodyguard."

Actually, he had both. And the babysitter could almost double as a bodyguard.

Colton ended the call. "Thanks for checking it out."

"No problem. It pays to be careful." Tanner's jaw tightened. "I have to admit, I spent most of my day off at your house."

Colton nodded. Tanner knew about someone tampering with Jasmine's car, but Paige probably hadn't told him she'd accosted the guy. And Colton wasn't about to spill any secrets. That was between Paige and Tanner. "Ready for that Ingles run?"

"Ready as I'll ever be. Swing around front, and I'll follow you."

Colton watched his friend head toward the steps leading down to Alpine and slid into the driver's seat. When he turned into Ingles's parking lot a short time later, the sky had darkened from gray to deep charcoal. He pulled into a space a short distance from one of the parking lot lights, and Tanner stopped next to him. By the time they finished their shopping, the darkness would be complete.

Colton snagged a cart and pulled out his cell phone. When he looked at his friend, Tanner had done the same thing.

Tanner held his up. "List from Paige."

He nodded. Jasmine had texted hers early that morning. At least Tanner was doing more than following him around the grocery store.

When they stepped back through the automatic doors a half hour later, each of their carts held four bags.

"That was relatively painless." Tanner's words held a touch of humor, but he didn't meet Colton's eyes. Instead, he scanned the parking lot, lines of concern on his face and tension radiating from him.

When they reached the SUV, Colton opened the back door.

Tanner passed him two of the bags. "Once we return the carts, I'm going to do a quick check of your vehicle again."

Colton nodded, his jaw tightening. It had been only four days since the note and the shot. Already that state of being constantly on guard was wearing on him.

When the last bag was loaded, he wheeled his cart toward the corral several spaces down, Tanner next to him. Away from the relative safety of his vehicle, a sense of vulnerability swept over him. Were his enemies out there somewhere, watching from the shadows?

He shook off the sensation. It was past dark, but the parking lot was well lit. It wasn't deserted, either. He wasn't the only one making an after-work stop before heading home.

He wheeled his cart between the parallel metal rails, then watched Tanner do the same. "Thanks for coming with me."

Tanner shrugged. "I had to come anyway. Besides, you're feeding me."

"Paige is feeding all five of us."

"With your food."

True. The ladies had planned it that morning, and Jasmine had informed him at lunchtime that they'd have company for dinner.

Tanner slid him a sideways glance. "Liam's starting to talk again."

"I know."

"Jasmine spent a lot of the day outside, but every time

she came back in, Liam seemed to light up. I think she's good for him."

Colton gave him a sharp look. What was he getting at? "She's his bodyguard. Liam getting attached to her isn't a good thing, because once this is over—"

Tanner's eyes dipped downward several inches and widened in a momentary flash of panic. Colton's words stuck in his throat.

The next moment, his muscled six-foot-two-inch friend slammed into him, knocking him to the asphalt behind the Highlander. Pain stabbed through his wrist and elbow.

"What—" He couldn't move. Tanner was on top of him, the injured arm pinned beneath him.

The weight lessened, then was gone.

"Stay low." Tanner hissed the words. "Get between the vehicles and call 911."

Colton's thoughts were spinning, but he forced himself into a crawl. When he put pressure on his left hand, the pain in his wrist intensified, and his arm buckled. Definitely sprained.

He finished the short trek in an awkward one-armed crawl. His elbow was on fire. He sank back on his heels and cupped it with the opposite hand. When he drew it away, blood dotted his palm. His suit coat was probably history. So was the dress shirt. The pants were likely shot, too, because now that he thought about it, his left knee had started to throb.

He unclipped his phone from his belt and looked for his friend. Tanner was positioned two feet away in a partial crouch, weapon drawn, peering through the Highlander's windows.

What had he seen?

No one had tried to shoot at them. There'd been no

crack of gunfire, not even the *pfsst* of a weapon with a silencer.

Colton dropped his gaze to his phone. It looked undamaged. Good thing he carried it on the right. Otherwise it might not have fared so well.

"What am I reporting?" All he knew was one of his best friends had just tackled him.

"I'm pretty sure someone aimed a rifle at you. I saw the red light of the laser on your chest."

Strength drained from Colton's body, and he leaned against his vehicle. If he'd been alone, chances were good he'd be dead right now.

Or maybe he wouldn't. Whoever was out there took aim but didn't pull the trigger. Maybe leveling that laser on his chest was part of the terror, one more way to make him crazy before delivering the final blow.

The scenario fit Perez perfectly. Once he had a target, he never lost interest until he'd seen his plans through to completion. Being on the receiving end of Perez's wrath was like walking around with a bomb strapped to one's chest.

For Colton, the timer had been triggered. It had happened the moment the jury delivered the verdict. Colton had put it on pause during his time at his in-laws'.

But the moment he came back to Atlanta, the countdown had resumed. And now nothing could stop it. Perez was likely orchestrating the whole thing from inside the maximum-security facility where he'd spend the rest of his life.

Through his goons on the outside, Perez would keep toying with him until he grew bored or decided Colton's time was up.

Then it would be over.

The clock would click to zero and...

Boom!

* * *

Jasmine stepped from the front deck into Colton's living room. This was the third time in the past twenty minutes.

Paige wasn't doing any better. She was pacing the living room with a whimpering Liam in her arms.

Jasmine shut and locked the door. "Any improvement?"

"He's burning up." Paige jiggled him, and Liam cried harder.

"Bryce should arrive with Colton any minute." Since nothing on Colton's schedule was to take him away from his desk, Tanner had dropped him off at the courthouse that morning, then headed to the station with plans to pick him up at the end of the day. But Liam had changed that.

He'd been fine when he'd gotten up. By late morning, he'd started to feel a little warm. When he threw up his lunch, she'd called Colton. Tanner was still at work, but since Bryce's shift wouldn't start until later, he'd agreed to shuttle Colton home.

Jasmine started her own pacing. Over the past thirty minutes, Liam's temperature had risen even more. Once Colton arrived, he'd decide how to proceed. Two days had passed since the incident in the Ingles parking lot, and nothing had happened since. But leaving the house with Liam made them all much more vulnerable.

Jasmine stepped back outside. Brutus stood at the bottom of the deck steps, stiff and alert. He'd apparently picked up on her tension.

When Bryce's Sorento came into view, she hurried to open the gate. As soon as the vehicle stopped, Colton jumped out and ran for the house, an elastic bandage peeking out from one jacket sleeve. All he'd gotten out of Tuesday night's scare was a sprained wrist and some asphalt scrapes.

"How's Liam?" He threw the words over his shoulder.

She hurried after him. "Really uncomfortable. His temperature has gone up a half degree since I called you."

Paige opened the door, still holding Liam. She'd apparently been watching for Colton and Bryce's return, too.

Jasmine followed him inside, Bryce right behind her. When Colton reached his son, he cupped the boy's face with both hands. "Liam, look at Daddy."

Panic laced his tone. Jasmine understood why. Liam had stopped fussing. Instead, he was listless, his eyes unfocused.

Colton ran to Liam's room and returned with a child-size afghan. "We're going to the emergency room."

Paige hesitated. "Shouldn't we call an ambulance?"

"I'd rather have armed escort." He wrapped the blanket around his son and took him from Paige.

Bryce unclipped his phone as they headed out the door. By the time Colton had fastened Liam into his car seat in the Highlander, Bryce had finished his conversation.

"A Cherokee County unit is headed this way."

Paige climbed in next to Liam, and Colton slid into the driver's seat. "We'll meet up on the four-lane."

Jasmine moved toward her own vehicle, calling instructions to Bryce as she walked. "Can you close the gate, then bring up the rear?"

The situation wasn't ideal. She'd feel better if they'd waited for Cherokee County. But even though Bryce was off duty, he was armed. He'd guaranteed them of that before he'd gone to pick up Colton. Of course, she was, too.

At the end of Hilltop, traffic was clear in both directions. She followed Colton through the left turn onto 64. Or "the four-lane," according to the locals. Since it

was the only four-lane road in all of Murphy, the name
worked.

She finished the turn and accelerated, checking her
rearview mirror. Bryce should catch up with them shortly.
She hoped he wasn't a slow driver. Colton had almost hit
the speed limit and was still accelerating.

On the right, A-1 Mini Storage came into view. An
older model Sunfire sat at an angle, as if ready to pull
out. She strained to see if the car was occupied, but the
windows were too tinted.

She shot past, then cast repeated glances in her rearview mirror. The car eased onto 64 and accelerated. Soon
it was gaining on her. Uneasiness trickled through her.

She moved into the left lane. She didn't want anyone
to get too close to Colton's Highlander, but if there was
a threat, she'd rather it be behind him than beside him.

When she checked again, a Sorento traveled some distance back. The Sunfire was gaining on her, but so was
Bryce. *Please hurry.*

As the small car drew closer to Colton's vehicle, Jasmine squeezed the wheel more tightly. Maybe the other
driver only wanted to get around her. She couldn't take
that chance. She was traveling just off Colton's left rear
quarter panel, the gap not large enough for another vehicle to fit between them.

The Sunfire disappeared from her rearview mirror
and appeared in her side mirror. It was now only two or
three car lengths from Colton's vehicle, close enough to
be considered tailgating.

The other car's engine revved, and the vehicle surged
forward. Jasmine glanced over her right shoulder, hoping
she was facing a case of road rage rather than a killer.

The rear window lowered, and in the midafternoon

sun, something metallic glinted. She did a double take, and her heart leaped into her throat.

The rear passenger held a pistol, and it was aimed at her.

She jammed on her brakes and jerked the wheel to the right. The crash of metal against metal reverberated through her vehicle, with the simultaneous explosion of the airbags. The impact set her spinning, tires making a shrill squeal that seemed to go on and on.

Don't roll the car, don't roll the car. She squeezed the wheel with every bit of strength she possessed, as if that would somehow keep all four tires on the pavement.

Over the top of the deflating airbags, trees whizzed past. She'd lost sight of the Sunfire. Colton's Highlander, too.

She slipped off the shoulder and bounced over the uneven surface, momentarily becoming airborne before hitting the ground with enough force to jar every bone in her body.

Through the front windshield, a stand of trees seemed to move toward her at lightning speed.

The next moment, her scream mingled with the sound of twisting metal and shattering glass.

Then everything fell silent.

Colton jammed on his brakes and pulled off the road, bouncing along the grassy shoulder until he came to a full stop. "Call 911. We need an ambulance."

He twisted in his seat to look at Liam. His eyes were closed. Was he asleep or unconscious?

"Make that two ambulances."

One would be for his son, the other for Jasmine. He didn't know her condition, but it didn't look good.

With his eyes on the road ahead of him, he hadn't

seen the crash. But he'd heard it and looked in the mirror in time to watch the car that had been tailgating him disappear off the road and Jasmine's Suburban begin a series of donuts. Now her vehicle was sitting thirty or forty feet behind him where a copse of trees had brought it to an abrupt stop. It rested at an angle, the windshield and driver window shattered.

God, please let her be okay. Please let Liam be okay.

Paige ended the call with the dispatcher and reached for the door handle. "Stay with Liam. I'll check on Jasmine."

Colton reached into the back seat and took his son's hand. Liam stirred. Though his eyelids lifted halfway, he didn't make eye contact. Colton's chest tightened. *God, please bring the ambulance quickly.*

He wouldn't remove his son from the car seat until the men who'd attacked Jasmine were in custody. Which should be soon. An SUV had turned around at a break in the median, a strobing light on its dash.

Some distance behind Jasmine's Suburban, the vehicle that had tailgated him sat with its front end wrapped around a tree, steam rising from beneath its hood. Bryce had stopped behind it and was approaching slowly, weapon raised.

Colton released Liam's hand to put the Highlander in Reverse and ease backward. Paige had reached Jasmine's SUV and was giving the driver door several hard yanks. He couldn't see well through the shattered glass, but there hadn't been any signs of movement.

Jasmine's driver door finally creaked open a foot. Paige gave it another forceful pull and it swung back fully.

When Colton eased up next to the Suburban, his heart almost stopped. Jasmine was slumped forward, head resting against the steering wheel. Two rivulets of blood traced paths down the side of her face.

As he lowered the passenger window, Paige reached into the vehicle and pressed her fingers against Jasmine's throat. She was checking for a pulse. *Dear God, she can't be...*

A lump formed in his throat. Jasmine would say putting her life in danger was part of the job. But she'd done this for him and his son. If anything happened to her, he'd never forgive himself.

A distant squeal pierced the silence. Paige put a hand on Jasmine's shoulder and murmured something to her. The soft timbre of her voice reached him, but not the words.

Colton killed the engine. When Jasmine lifted her head, he released a breath he hadn't realized he'd been holding. *Thank You, Lord.*

She rubbed the back of her neck, then stiffened. "Liam—"

"—is safe." Paige straightened. "You should stay put. There's an ambulance on the way."

"No." She released the seat belt and struggled to her feet. Once standing, she put a hand on her weapon and swayed. "I need to check on Liam."

"You need to sit." Paige grasped her arm and helped her into the Highlander's back seat.

Jasmine took Liam's hands in hers. "He needs a doctor. He's burning up."

"Help is on the way."

She leaned back against the seat, the tension draining out of her.

Colton studied her. Her head was cut and bleeding. She also likely had a concussion. But there apparently weren't any broken bones.

"What happened? Did he hit you?"

"I hit him…after I saw the passenger had a pistol pointed at me."

Colton's gut filled with lead. The gunman had intended to take out Jasmine to get to him.

A shout from Bryce drew Colton's attention toward the Sunfire. He still stood facing the car, his posture stiff, weapon trained on the man in the back seat. "Hands in the air."

For several tense moments, Bryce didn't move. Colton held his breath. He couldn't see into the car at that distance, but he had a good idea of what was going on. According to Jasmine, the man had aimed a pistol at her. That weapon was somewhere inside.

The sirens grew closer, and Colton looked toward town. Flashing blue lights appeared around a gentle bend in the road. Two ambulances trailed behind.

The sheriff cruiser flew past, then turned around at the first break in the median. After stopping behind the wrecked Sunfire, a deputy jumped out. Bryce gestured toward the rear driver's-side door, and the deputy swung it open, weapon pointed inside. After pulling a cloth from his back pocket, he reached in and removed a pistol.

When Colton looked at Jasmine again, her hands had fallen into her lap and her head was tipped back against the seat. Her eyes were closed.

"Hey, don't go to sleep."

She roused herself to look at him. It seemed to take a lot of effort.

"You've probably got a concussion." He glanced back up the four-lane, where the ambulances were completing their U-turn. "Help will be here in a minute."

"No, I don't need to go to the hospital. It's just a bump

on the head." She touched the side of her face. When she saw blood smearing her palm, her eyes widened.

"You've got to go, let them check you out."

She touched her head again. "This is nothing. Head wounds always bleed profusely. A wet cloth and a couple of Band-Aids, and I'll be fine. I just need rest."

Colton heaved a sigh. He'd never gone head-to-head with Jasmine. She definitely had a stubborn streak.

"If you won't listen to me, maybe you'll listen to someone else." He snatched his phone from his side and pulled up his contacts. Burch Security's administrative assistant answered after the first ring. A half minute later, Colton had Gunter Burch on the line.

After briefly relaying what had happened, he looked at Jasmine. "She got seriously whacked in the head and is insisting she's fine. I think she needs some tough love." He handed Jasmine his phone.

After a brief pause, Jasmine spoke. "Colton's exaggerating. I've got a few cuts, nothing that can't be remedied with some butterfly bandages." Another pause. "So I'll have a headache. I'm not confused. I know my name and my address and what day it is. I can even go into all kinds of detail about my overprotective boss, who's under the deluded assumption that he's been commissioned to play the role of my father."

Colton bit back a smile.

Finally, Jasmine heaved a sigh. "Okay, I'll get checked out."

She ended the call, then frowned at the phone before handing it back to him. "I hate hospitals."

"They'll just look at you, probably run some tests. They may not even keep you overnight."

"They'd better not."

She unfastened the straps on Liam's car seat and pulled

him onto her lap. For several moments, she held him close, rubbing his back with one hand. Emergency medical personnel would soon take him away from her. One ambulance had stopped behind the Highlander and two paramedics were moving their direction. The other ambulance was parked near the Sunfire.

When Jasmine's gaze met Colton's, it held a softness he'd never seen. Her guard was down, every barrier crumbled. Emotion rushed through him with the force of a tidal wave.

She'd risked her life to save his and Liam's. She could have simply evaded the men, but slamming into them ensured they wouldn't be able to reach him and his son.

And he'd almost lost her.

A black hole opened up inside him. It was more than guilt, deeper than a feeling of responsibility.

He closed his eyes, trying to get a grip on his runaway emotions. This couldn't be happening. He couldn't be falling for his son's bodyguard.

The job was ending. The men who'd threatened them for the past three weeks were heading to the hospital for treatment, then straight to jail. It was time for Jasmine to go back to Atlanta and move on to her next assignment.

He tried to tell himself that was okay. He wasn't looking for someone to replace Mandy. If he was, it wouldn't be Jasmine. Not that she wouldn't make a great wife for someone. She would. But she wasn't his type.

He wasn't hers, either. Young and full of life, she'd probably go for someone more like his fun-loving brother.

He stepped from the vehicle to meet the paramedics. His mental arguments were logical. Persuasive.

Of course they were. That was his specialty. He could convince judges and sway jurors with his words.

But his own heart wasn't even listening.

EIGHT

Jasmine stepped out the double doors of MountainView Community Church and squinted in the midday sunshine. Liam was in her arms, Colton behind her carrying their coats. The temperature had risen considerably since early that morning.

Liam was a different boy than he'd been three days earlier. He'd been treated in the emergency room, then released once his temperature had come down to a less scary level. He'd had a bad virus. Fortunately, it was the twenty-four-hour kind, or more like thirty-six hours. He'd gotten up yesterday morning ready to play between naps. This morning he'd insisted on going to church.

Her own emergency room visit hadn't gone as well as Liam's had. The doctor had been concerned about the possibility of a concussion and ordered a CAT scan. The cuts had needed nothing more than butterfly bandages. But the visit had evolved into an overnight stay, and it had been late in the day Friday before she'd been able to convince everyone she was fine.

Andi slipped a hand into Bryce's. "See you at our place in a few."

They'd talked yesterday about the seven of them, Paige and Tanner included, having Sunday dinner in town, then decided instead to do a cookout at Bryce's. For the time being, everyone was remaining on alert. The men who'd threatened them on the highway were in custody. They weren't Perez's brothers, according to their identification. Of course, those names could be aliases.

After strapping Liam into his car seat, Jasmine climbed into the front. Colton cranked the engine and glanced over at her. "I'm glad you sat with us today."

She shrugged. Liam hadn't given her a choice. Instead of going to children's church, he'd insisted on sitting with the "big people." In Liam's mind, "big people" had included her. As Colton had carried him down the aisle, he'd stretched out his arms and pleaded in that sweet little voice, "I want Jasmine." How was she supposed to resist that?

So she'd sat in the third row, nestled between Liam and Paige, Colton on his son's other side. Sitting that close to the worship band, the song lyrics and the meaning behind them had been hard to ignore. And too many times, she'd found the pastor's message unsettling.

As expected, it had a Christmas theme—"Emmanuel, God with Us." He made it relevant to today by talking about God's presence through the storms of life. But she wasn't looking for a God who promised to be with her through the storms. She wanted to avoid them altogether.

Colton drove down the steep drive, then smiled over at her. "You look like you're deep in thought."

She tilted her head to the side. "Do you believe God saw your wife's aneurysm before it ruptured?"

"Of course He did." He stepped on the gas, pulling onto Fall Branch Road. "Nothing catches Him by surprise."

"Then why didn't he do anything to stop it? He's all-powerful, right? He could have intervened but chose not to."

"I don't have all the answers. But I do know God is right here and will carry me through whatever trials I have to face."

Jasmine chewed her lower lip. She'd never experienced that kind of faith. But something told her if she ever found it, the peace she'd sought all her life might be somewhere in the midst of it.

Colton eased to a stop at the end of the road, then turned right toward 64. "I'm not saying it's been easy. It hasn't. Losing Mandy is one of the hardest things I've ever experienced, right up there with losing my mother."

"And you believe God has helped you through it."

He nodded. "I have no doubt. I've felt His presence, seen Him at work."

"How?"

For several moments, he didn't respond. The light ahead turned red, and he eased to a stop. When he finally looked at her, his eyes were serious, filled with meaning. "Most recently? I asked for someone big and mean and scary, and He sent me you."

The words floored her. "You think God sent me?"

"Absolutely." He craned his neck to look at his son in the rearview mirror. "Look at the change that's happened in Liam in three short weeks."

The light changed and Colton stepped on the gas. "You were exactly what he needed. I didn't know that, but God did."

She swallowed hard. He'd said she was what Liam needed. What about what Colton needed?

"So you believe God orchestrated events so I'd be the one to guard you two."

"Without a doubt."

She shook her head. "If He did all that, why not just

seal up the aneurysm? Then the other stuff wouldn't have been necessary."

"Sometimes God stills the storm, like He did for the disciples on the Sea of Galilee. Other times He carries us through it."

"Like He did for Paul and the other two-hundred-something passengers on the ship that wrecked." She'd been listening. If she thought about it, she could probably even recite several of the pastor's sermon points.

She crossed her arms. "The whole thing bugs me."

"What bugs you?"

"How all this works. I mean, you're a nice guy, a family man, church attender, a good, moral person. If God should spare anyone from having to go through something horrible, I would think it would be someone like you."

"That's not the way life works. At least not *this* life."

And now he was going to tell her he had heaven to look forward to. Jasmine frowned. She'd always believed in an afterlife, but heaven had never felt real. It seemed more the stuff of fairy tales, a way to explain death to a child.

But when she looked over at Colton, he was well-grounded. That peace she coveted was evident on his face, along with a genuine acceptance of his circumstances. But there was more than that. A sense of contentment seemed to weave through his whole being.

He pulled up to his gate a short time later. "Stay with Liam. I'll run in and get the potato salad." That would be their contribution to the meal.

Brutus met Colton at the gate, wagging his tail. Although he was still playing the part of guard dog, he was getting to spend more time inside the house, and not just when the weather was bad. Though he'd tear apart anyone who threatened his pack, his gentleness with Liam warmed her heart.

After giving the dog two pats on the head, Colton jogged toward the house. Jasmine stepped from the SUV and scanned the surrounding woods, leaving the door open.

Liam's voice came from inside the vehicle. "Jasmine?"

She leaned inside. "Jasmine's right here, sweetie. I'm not going anywhere."

Her assurances seemed to satisfy him. How was he going to handle it when she finally left for good? A vise clamped down on her chest.

That day was coming. Soon. Colton didn't seem to be in any hurry to send her back to Atlanta. And she wasn't in any hurry to go. Waiting to find out who the men were and why they'd attacked was a great reason to extend the assignment. Their names weren't familiar to Colton. And neither of them was talking.

But detectives were working on it. Eventually they'd find the connection, and Colton would have to decide whether he and his son still needed her protection.

She turned in a slow circle, scanning her surroundings. She'd been identifying and guarding against threats for enough years to have developed a sixth sense. Now there was nothing, not even a blip on her radar. The danger here was over.

Colton stepped out the front door, then locked the dead bolt with the key. He was still taking precautions and probably would for the rest of his life. The experiences he'd had tended to leave a permanent mark.

He closed the gate, and she climbed back into the SUV. After sliding into the driver's seat, he handed her the cold container. He'd said he'd pick up some potato salad somewhere. She'd insisted his friends deserved homemade.

"I've enjoyed getting to know Paige this week."

Colton smiled. "I'm glad you two hit it off so well."

Although she didn't know Paige's whole story, she'd learned enough to know they had a lot in common, including their dysfunctional childhoods. As adults, they shared that toughness that only comes with the struggle to survive. It wouldn't take much for them to become best friends.

There was one difference between them, though. After a bunch of bad relationships, Paige had found the love of her life in Tanner.

Jasmine wasn't there yet. She had the bad relationship part down pat, but finding true love seemed more of a distant dream.

She slid a sideways glance toward Colton. His eyes were on the road ahead of him as he drove down Hilltop toward the four-lane. The tightness that his features had held since the day she met him had disappeared.

She'd found him attractive from the moment he'd walked up her driveway and insisted on helping her haul in buckets of paint. But his appeal went much deeper than his physical attractiveness.

He was kind, compassionate and selfless, the type of man who'd do anything for those he loved. He didn't project the carefree abandon that his brother always seemed to display, but that wasn't what drew her to him. He had depth, integrity. Even his faith tugged at her in a way she hadn't expected.

What would it be like to be a permanent part of Colton's and Liam's lives? Was there even the slightest possibility that she could find with him what Paige had experienced with Tanner?

Colton braked at the stop sign at the end of Hilltop

and looked over at her. His lips lifted in an amused smile. He'd caught her staring at him.

"And what are you thinking about now?"

Heat crept up her cheeks. No way was she going to admit the direction her thoughts had taken. Not only were her feelings for him unprofessional, putting them out there would make the rest of their interactions stiff and uncomfortable.

She shrugged. "I was thinking about how much more relaxed you look."

Not a lie. In fact, that was the observation that had started her whole train of thought.

His smile deepened as he turned onto 64. "I'm *feeling* more relaxed. I'm not ready to totally let down my guard, but I'm not expecting someone to start shooting at me, either."

He cast her a quick glance. "I owe you a lot."

Their eyes had met for the briefest of moments, but the sincerity in his sent a surge of warmth through her insides. She shrugged. "Just doing my job."

"You saved our lives, probably more than once. I want you to know how much I appreciate everything you've done."

When he stopped in Bryce's driveway a minute or so later, his phone was ringing. He frowned down at a number he apparently didn't recognize. Moments after answering, the frown gave way to eagerness.

When he ended the call, he clipped the phone back onto his belt.

She looked at him with raised brows. "That sounded like good news."

He nodded. "Perez was behind the attacks. The guys had several aliases, but they're his brothers."

"Do the detectives think there are others out there who want to see you dead?"

"No one can say for sure, but Perez doesn't have any other relatives. Male ones, anyway. His father was killed by rival gang members when Perez was a boy, and he doesn't have any other brothers."

"Friends, acquaintances?"

"As near as they can tell, none close enough to put their own lives in jeopardy to do his dirty work. So it looks like, starting tomorrow, you'll be able to go back home and move on to your next assignment."

Jasmine studied him as he spoke. Did his shoulders slouch a little? No, that was her imagination. The news he'd gotten was cause for celebration.

He pulled the keys from the ignition. "Today you're still on duty. And your assignment for the rest of the afternoon is to relax and have fun getting to know my friends."

He stepped from the SUV, then leaned into the back to unbuckle Liam. "Are you ready to go in and see Aunt Andi and Uncle Bryce?" His tone was cheery. But it seemed forced.

Maybe he *would* be sad to see her go. Was it possible he was feeling at least some of what she'd been fighting?

No, she needed to stop trying to see things that weren't there. Colton was still mourning the loss of his wife. And he wasn't looking for a replacement. Even if he were, she'd never be able to fill Mandy's shoes.

Perfect wife and perfect mother. She and Colton had probably had a near perfect marriage.

Jasmine had never even had a dating relationship that didn't fall squarely into the realm of dysfunctional. If she couldn't make men who were as messed up as she was happy, how would she have any hope of making

Colton happy when she had to follow in the footsteps of a woman like Mandy?

She climbed from the SUV and walked with Colton toward the porch. This afternoon, she was going to do exactly what he'd ordered—relax and have a good time with his friends.

Tomorrow she'd head back to Atlanta. If Gunn didn't have an immediate assignment, maybe she could get the work finished at the house. She'd been close when she'd had to pull off for the Gale assignment.

Maybe she could convince Gunn to give her the last two weeks of the vacation she'd earned. She'd again pour her time and energy into making the reality of her new house match the pictures she'd conjured in her mind. It would be fun watching it take shape and all come together.

She heaved a sigh. All her efforts to rouse some enthusiasm for her plans fell flat.

That was because everything she looked forward to involved leaving the man who made her dream of things she'd thought impossible and the little boy who'd stolen her heart.

Liam sat on the floor amid scattered toys and crumpled wrapping paper. Behind him, several hundred mini lights shone from the tree.

There was still one wrapped gift lying beneath. It had Jasmine's name on it. After the cookout at Bryce's, she'd packed her belongings and Colton had driven her back to Atlanta. He should have given it to her then, but he'd forgotten.

Or maybe the oversight was a subconscious effort to make sure he'd have to see her again.

He rose from the floor, where he'd helped Liam open

his gifts, and collected the discarded paper. It was his first Christmas without Mandy, Liam's first without his mother.

But it wasn't Mandy that Liam had been asking for.

It was Jasmine.

At least, he'd asked for her Sunday night and most of the day yesterday. By last night, he'd stopped. Because he'd stopped talking altogether.

This was what he'd been afraid of. He hadn't wanted his son getting attached to her. But it had happened anyway. And now Liam had lost a second mother figure.

After throwing away the paper, he returned to the living room and stared out the front window. The sun was still low on the horizon, hidden behind the trees. He moved away and squatted next to his son. "How about some breakfast?"

Liam loaded a double handful of plastic rocks onto the dump truck without looking up. When he pressed the button on the side, the bed rose and the rocks tumbled onto the rug.

Colton tried again. "We'll have pancakes, your favorite."

Liam's eyes met his, and his chest clenched at the vacancy he saw there.

He ruffled Liam's hair. "I'll make you a Mickey Mouse one. Would you like that?"

Liam nodded, and Colton rose. On his way through the room, he stopped at the coffee table. A sterling silver bookmark lay on the polished oak surface, engraved with the words *Keep the Faith*.

When he'd pulled Liam's gifts out from beneath the tree, he'd found a small wrapped box with his name on it. The tag said, "Thanks for letting me be a part of your family. Jaz."

Since she'd spent most of the past two weeks seques-
tered in the house with Liam, she had to have gotten
some help. Probably from Paige. That made the gift all
the more thoughtful.

He was going to miss her. Actually, he'd started missing her five minutes after she left. Her going home didn't
just leave a hole in his son's life. It also left a hole in his
own.

He trudged into the kitchen. No need to feign the excitement he was trying to display for his son's benefit.
He plugged in the griddle and pulled the pancake mix
from the cupboard. An easy meal.

Christmas dinner was going to be even more effort-
less. It was in the fridge, waiting to be moved to the
oven and warmed. He'd picked it up at Ingles yesterday.
Instead of turkey, he'd selected a Cornish game hen. A
ten-pound turkey was a little overkill for one man and a
thirty-pound boy.

But it was going to be just the two of them. Bryce and
Andi were having Christmas dinner with Andi's family
in Asheville, and Tanner and Paige, both without any
real family connections, had left yesterday morning for
a week in a Florida beach condo.

Not that he hadn't had other invitations. He had.
Mandy's parents had invited him to spend the holidays
in Montana. His own had asked him to come to New
York to be with them and his grandparents. He'd even
gotten invitations from a couple of his Atlanta friends,
the most insistent coming from his former coworker
Doug.

As Colton added the wet ingredients, sounds of play
came from the living room. There was no chatter, or
vocalizing of any kind, just the hum of the mechanism

that raised the dump truck bed and the muffled clatter of plastic rocks.

Colton had just ladled the first spoonful of batter onto the griddle when his phone rang. Doug's voice came through the line, a little subdued.

"I'm hesitant to wish you a merry Christmas, but I'm praying it's a little easier than we'd expect."

"Thanks." He added two dollops of batter to the larger one to form Mickey's ears. "At least I no longer have someone trying to kill me." He'd spoken with Doug while Jasmine was still in the hospital, letting him know what had happened.

"That should make for at least a little Christmas cheer. Have you learned who they were?"

"Perez's brothers."

"Oh, no. How—"

The line went silent. "Doug?"

When his friend spoke, his voice was tight. "Did you get a gift basket delivery a few days after you left?"

"No. Why?"

"I might know how they found you. Friday, I got a card in the mail from the victim's family in a case I just tried, thanking me for all my efforts. A new intern we have was there when I opened it. He said we probably get that a lot."

Doug drew in a deep breath and continued. "He said someone tried to deliver one of those candy-and-nut gift baskets to you three weeks or so ago. When he said you were no longer working there, the delivery person asked if he knew where you'd gone. He said he thought you'd gone to Cherokee County, North Carolina, but wasn't sure."

Colton leaned against the counter, the pieces falling into place. No wonder they'd found him so quickly. The first time he'd left, it had been different. Most of the office staff knew where he'd gone, but even if that information had gotten back to Perez, his brothers had probably decided against following him to Montana, knowing he'd be back eventually.

Colton created another Mickey Mouse, then started four more pancakes cooking, boring round ones. By the time the conversation was winding down, all six were golden brown and stacked on two plates.

Doug sighed. "Are you sure you don't want to spend the day in Atlanta? We'd love for you to join us."

"Thanks, but we're just going to have a quiet Christmas at home."

Doug came from a big family. At last count, there were going to be thirty people at his gathering. That was more chaos than Colton wanted to deal with.

After ending the call, he opened the fridge to remove the maple syrup from the door. Three covered containers sat on the second shelf. Christmas dinner.

He'd turned down Doug's invitation because a gathering with thirty-plus people had sounded more grueling than fun. But three would be perfect.

He walked back to the counter where he'd left his phone. Jasmine didn't have plans. He'd already asked what she was going to be doing. She'd reiterated that she'd never been big on holiday celebrations.

She answered after three rings, sounding a little breathless. She was apparently happy to hear from him. Or maybe she'd had to run for the phone.

Whatever her reason, everything inside him responded to her sweet voice. They'd agreed to keep in touch, but he hadn't spoken with her since he and Liam had said goodbye to her Sunday night.

Now something tugged at him, the longing to be with

her again, even if only for the day. Maybe it would help Liam. Maybe he needed regular visits to know that Jasmine wasn't gone like Mandy.

He cleared his throat. "What are you up to?"

"Painting."

"That's dedication. Liam and I haven't even eaten breakfast yet."

"What are you having?"

"Pancakes, complete with mouse ears. His, anyway."

"You're a good dad." There was a smile in her tone.

It tugged one out of him. "Thanks. How about doing a late Christmas dinner with us?"

"In Murphy?"

"No, I'll bring it to you. You'll just have to walk across the street."

"That sounds good. I'd love to see Liam again."

"What about his grumpy father?"

"Him, too."

"It's not going to feel like Christmas. There won't be any decorations."

"At least the company will be good."

"We'll try. I'm afraid you won't get much interaction out of Liam, though." He drew in a breath and released it in a sigh. "He's regressed. As of last night, he's completely stopped talking again."

"Oh, no. I was afraid of that." She paused. "If you want to maintain regular contact, I don't mind. If we FaceTimed or Skyped on a regular basis, that might help him adjust."

He closed his eyes, that tug stronger than ever. Jasmine was a special person. The assignment was over. She owed them nothing more. But she was willing to do whatever she could to help ease Liam into the next phase of his life.

After settling on a time for dinner, he disconnected

the call and carried plates and utensils to the table. Last was the maple syrup and a milk-filled sippy cup.

When he returned to the living room, the dump truck was parked, and his son was playing with a set of Lincoln Logs.

"Are you ready to eat?"

Liam didn't look up.

"We need to eat our breakfast. Then we're going to have dinner with Miss Jasmine."

Liam's head swiveled toward him. Hope filled his eyes and his mouth lifted in a one-sided smile.

Colton scooped him up and walked to the kitchen. His son wasn't the only one whose day had gotten brighter. Colton was now looking forward to a meal he'd dreaded for the past two days.

He put Liam in the high chair and placed his plate on the tray. Although Liam eyed the pancakes hungrily, he waited until Colton sat, then held out his hands. When Colton had finished praying, Liam's eyes met his.

And they held life.

As Colton cut the Mickey Mouse pancakes into bite-size pieces, his stomach twisted in a mixture of anguish and hope. For almost seven months, he'd tried to be everything for his son. But it wasn't enough. Liam needed more.

He needed Jasmine.

As long as she was willing, Colton would see to it that they maintained regular contact. He'd drive to Atlanta on weekends and holidays. During the week and anytime he couldn't make it, they'd FaceTime or Skype.

Anything to help ease Liam's loneliness.

But what about his own?

NINE

Colton opened the oven door and a blast of heat hit him in the face. Cartoon voices drifted in to him from the living room, where Liam was occupied with *Rudolph the Red-Nosed Reindeer*. Jasmine would arrive in thirty minutes. They'd scheduled Christmas dinner for three to give her extra time to paint.

Satisfied that the food was progressing as it should, he closed the oven door and walked from the room. When he entered the living room, Liam was standing at the front window, vertical blind slats resting on each shoulder, head holding them apart. He seemed to have been watching for Jasmine almost from the moment they arrived. Colton had lost count of how many times Liam had run to the window to peer out, then returned to the movie.

"Dinner isn't ready yet, but when it is, she'll be here." He carried Liam to the couch and settled in next to him. The movie continued to play, and he hugged his son close, a sense of contentment swelling inside. *Thank You, God.* He'd brought them through a scary time. They still had healing to do. And Jasmine's place in their futures was a big unknown. But they were safe.

The ringtone sounded on his phone. Rather than trying to talk over *Rudolph*, he strode into the kitchen to take the call. It was Jasmine. When she spoke, she sounded breathless. "I just finished the living room, which was a chore with the cathedral ceilings."

"At least you got your workout today."

She groaned. "Stretches, check. Quads, check. And a few other muscles I didn't know I had, check, check and check. I'm going to feel this tomorrow."

"I can imagine." Although, she was probably exaggerating. As physically fit as she was, her body likely wouldn't even register the additional activity. Jasmine was no couch potato.

"Anyhow, I'm running about twenty minutes late. I've got to clean my brush and rollers and then myself." The humor returned to her voice. "I'm a three-coat painter—one on the wall, one on the floor and one on me."

He laughed. "Take your time. Liam is occupied with Christmas movies, and I can always turn the temperature down on the oven."

He laid the phone on the counter and removed a glass from the cupboard. After filling it with ice, he poured some of the sweetened tea he'd picked up yesterday.

When he returned to his spot on the couch, he kissed Liam on the head and gave him another squeeze. For the next several minutes, he sipped his tea while watching the animated movie.

Rudolph had just been chosen to be the head reindeer guiding the sleigh. The turning point. The start of the happy ending. Was there one in store for him and his son? Actually, they'd had one, with the arrest of the Perez brothers. But what about the hole that Mandy's death had left in their lives?

Whenever he tried to envision that happy ending, Jasmine figured prominently in every image. He'd already decided to maintain regular contact. And she'd agreed.

But Liam didn't just need occasional visits. He needed a constant in his life. Someone to kiss away the boo-boos with the tenderness that only a woman could provide. Someone to hold and comfort him after a nightmare. He needed a mother.

And Colton needed more than a friend. The loneliness had been more acute in the past two days than it had in several months. He'd gotten used to having Jasmine around and never dreamed that the house would feel so empty without her.

Now that the assignment was over, their relationship had moved easily from strictly professional to friends. Was there any chance it could move from friends to something deeper?

He couldn't deny the attraction he felt. She was completely different from Mandy, but every bit as beautiful. He already respected and admired her. Strong in spite of a fractured past. Tough when needed, but surprisingly tender. Caring and selfless, putting others' needs above her own. It wouldn't take much for the admiration and respect he felt to grow into love.

Jasmine would be an amazing mother to Liam. And a good wife to him.

The thought was like having a bucket of cold water thrown in his face. He rose from the couch and started to pace. Over the past few minutes, he'd taken the leap from being glad they could visit regularly to thinking about making her his wife. How had that happened?

He stopped in the foyer and leaned against the front door. What he was thinking wasn't even practical. Jasmine liked him as a friend, and she'd connected with his son in a powerful and unexpected way. But she'd never hinted at feeling any kind of attraction toward him.

He returned to the living room in time to see Liam

disappear into the hall, headed toward his room. He'd apparently lost interest in the movie.

Colton continued to pace. Once he got used to Jasmine not being there and they settled into the routine of regular visits, he'd get his head back on straight. It was just that the loneliness was getting to him. The time of year didn't help, either—the holidays with their constant focus on family, the continual reminders of what was missing in his life.

He walked into the foyer again and paused. Did he just hear the kitchen door rattle? He couldn't have. Brutus had been inside with them earlier, but Colton had let him out an hour ago to do his business and enjoy the outdoors. As long as he was outside, no one would get anywhere near the house.

Unless they had a tranquilizer dart.

His gut filled with lead. Perez's brothers were off the street. But what if there was someone else?

His eyes went to the alarm panel two feet to his right, and he pressed the button to arm the system. When he reached for his phone, he winced. He'd never picked it back up after pouring his tea.

The next moment, the sharp snap of splitting wood sent a bolt of panic through him. Someone had just kicked in the back door. The ear-piercing squeal of the alarm filled the house, setting his teeth on edge.

He ran toward the back, reaching the living room the same time two men entered from the direction of the kitchen. A sick sense of déjà vu swept over him. Two men in ski masks and gloves. One larger and one smaller.

He continued his panicked dash into the hall. He had to get to Liam before they did. The police would have already been notified. The alarm was still monitored. He just had to hang on until they arrived.

But Jasmine would get there sooner. She was probably already in action. She'd have heard the squeal of the alarm from across the street, grabbed her weapon and dashed out the door.

As he ran down the hall, heavy footsteps pounded behind him. He'd just bolted through his son's door when a large body crashed into him, tackling him from behind. He hit the floor, his assailant landing on top of him. The impact knocked the air from his lungs, and he struggled in a constricted breath.

Liam released a terrified scream as piercing as the wail of the alarm. The man rolled Colton onto his back while the second man entered the room. Colton twisted, reaching for his son. A meaty fist moved toward the side of his face at lightning speed, connecting almost before the threat registered. Stars exploded across his vision.

The thinner man lifted Liam from the floor and Colton struggled to rise. But the larger man tightened his hold, keeping him pinned to the floor.

As the man carrying Liam moved past him, Colton lifted an arm toward his son. "No."

The word sounded far away, as if it came from somewhere else. Someone was taking his son, and there was no one to stop him. Why hadn't Jasmine come?

Suddenly he was free. He rolled onto his stomach, then rose to his hands and knees. Blackness encroached from all directions, and a watery weakness filled his limbs.

He lifted one knee, placing that foot flat on the floor. He couldn't let the men take his son. He had to get up.

He reached for Liam's dresser, but his perception was off. His hand found nothing but air. A boot met his ribs, and pain shot through his side. The blow knocked him back onto the floor. The men disappeared from the room.

He pushed himself back into a crawling position. He

couldn't lose consciousness. He had to save his son. *God, please help me.*

He forced a hand forward, then a knee, then the other hand, rotating his body as he moved. The open doorway was in front of him. Inch by inch he crawled through, his circle of vision growing smaller by the second. The alarm still squealed, but there was another squeal, even closer. It was inside his head.

He flopped onto his side, the last vestiges of consciousness slipping away.

He'd made a terrible mistake. The capture of Perez's brothers wasn't the end. There were other men determined to bring him down.

Men every bit as dangerous.

And now they had Liam.

A roar filled the bathroom, and Jasmine's hair danced in the hot stream of air coming from the blow-dryer.

Before cleaning her brushes and rollers, she'd set the light/heater/exhaust fan combo to heat. So the room had been warm and cozy by the time she'd stepped into the shower.

Now she was dressed in a sweater and a nice pair of jeans. She didn't have a Christmas sweater, or even any holiday jewelry, but this one was at least red.

She pressed the off switch and laid the blow-dryer on the counter, then fluffed her hair with her fingers. She hadn't always worn it short. When she was a teenager, it had hung almost to her waist. As a young adult, she'd worn it shoulder length. While deployed, she'd wanted easy. Wash and wear. The style had stuck.

A lot of men liked long, flowing locks. Fortunately, she wasn't looking to please any men.

After winding up the cord on the blow-dryer, she

dropped it into one of the vanity drawers. Eventually it would hang on the back of the bathroom door. Once she got a hook installed. One of many small projects still undone.

She took a final look in the mirror, then reached for the heater switch. She was ready except for putting on her boots. And it was five minutes earlier than the estimate she'd given Colton.

When she flipped the switch, the heater motor died. But she didn't get the silence she'd expected. There seemed to be a faint squeal coming from somewhere else in the house.

She frowned. What was she hearing? She opened the bathroom door and moved through her room, down the hall and into the living room.

The squeal was louder now. A siren? No, the pitch was too constant. It was more like an alarm.

Colton's alarm.

When she swung open the front door, she had no doubt. The shrill squeal was coming from across the street.

She raced to retrieve her weapon from where she'd laid it on her nightstand, but didn't take the time to don her jacket or her boots. Seconds later, she was running down her driveway in her stockinged feet, weapon stuck into the waistband of her jeans.

Colton's driveway was empty, the front gate still closed. His own vehicle was likely parked in the garage. Law enforcement hadn't responded yet. So maybe the alarm had been triggered right before she shut off the bathroom heater. Whoever had tripped it could still be inside.

She pulled out her weapon and slipped through the

gate. Brutus didn't come to greet her. And he wasn't barking.

A sick sense of dread wrapped around her.

What if the men who'd tried to kidnap Liam weren't the same two who'd come after them in Murphy?

What if they'd let down their guard too soon?

She crept closer to the house, every sense on full alert. When she stepped onto the porch, she tried the door. Locked. None of the windows appeared to have been tampered with, either.

She moved across the front, rounded the corner and walked along the side. When she stepped into the back, she picked up her pace. Something didn't look right. A dark shape stood out at the base of the shrubs lining the rear wall.

Brutus. Now she had no doubt. That dark, unmoving blob was the dog, likely the victim of another tranquilizer dart.

Which meant Liam's kidnappers had returned.

Her gut burned with a cocktail of worry and fear. As she crept along the back of the house, another sound seemed to blend with the screech of the alarm, the pitch rising and falling. Help should be there within minutes. But Colton and Liam might not have that long.

She approached the kitchen door. It was open. The side of the jamb that was visible from her vantage point was splintered. Everything inside her demanded that she rush through, shouting Colton's name. Instead, she shut down her emotions and called on her extensive training. She couldn't lose her wits now.

She tiptoed toward the door, shifting to a crouch at each window. When she reached the nearest edge of the doorway, she stopped. A moment later, she leaped across the opening to disappear behind the opposite side, weapon still raised. During that brief span of time, she'd taken in the view of the kitchen and dining area. No one was there.

She jumped through the doorway and spun around the edge of the kitchen counter, then cleared each area the same way. The living room offered an unobstructed view down the hall, where a crumpled form lay half in, half out of Liam's bedroom.

Once again, she had to corral her feelings. Heedlessly rushing in could get her killed. She stood frozen for several moments, listening. But the wailing alarm drowned out any possible sounds of movement inside the house.

So did the sirens. They were closer now, probably right at the entrance to the subdivision. In another half minute or so, backup would arrive. In the meantime, Colton's life could be ebbing away. And she still didn't know Liam's whereabouts.

Colton stirred and released a moan. Relief shot through her. He was hurt, but he was alive.

He pushed himself to a seated position but didn't try to rise. As she rushed toward him, conflicting emotions flitted across his face—relief mixed with agony. "They took Liam."

"Who?"

"The same men as before. I don't know. They had ski masks." He grimaced and pressed a hand to the side of his head. "The alarm."

"What's your code?"

"Nine-four-three-six."

As she made her way to the front of the house, sirens rose in volume, then fell abruptly silent. She'd just punched in the four numbers when a loud knock sounded on the front door.

She swung it open. Two Atlanta police officers stood

on Colton's front porch. She invited them in and told them what she knew, which wasn't much.

When she led them into the hall, Colton was rising, clinging to the doorjamb for support. "They took my son."

He stood shaking his head, his shoulders hunched. He wasn't just hurt. He was defeated. Her heart clenched.

The older of the two officers spoke. Posner, according to his nameplate. "Did you see which way they went?"

"No. The bigger guy knocked me out."

Jasmine stepped forward. "Since the front door was still locked, they probably left the same way they came in—through the back. Then over the wall with the help of the oak tree."

The younger officer took off in that direction while Officer Posner spoke into his radio. When he'd finished calling for backup and instructing them to comb the woods behind the subdivision, he turned to Colton again.

"Any idea who these men were?"

"No."

"Or what they want?"

"My son, but I don't know why. This is their second visit. The first time they weren't successful."

Over the next hour, several people were in and out of Colton's house, including two detectives. Since the men had worn gloves, the detectives had decided against dusting for prints.

Liam's information was going immediately into the missing persons database. Soon his photo would be all over Atlanta and beyond, disseminated throughout the law enforcement agencies.

At one point, Jasmine had found Colton texting both Tanner and Bryce, asking them to pray for Liam's return. The extra prayers wouldn't hurt. But she didn't put much confidence in them. If God intended to offer any kind of intervention on Liam's or Colton's behalf, He'd have prevented the kidnapping to begin with.

Finally, she and Colton were alone in the living room. Christmas dinner was still in the oven. She'd turned it off after the police arrived, but it was probably too dried-up to eat. Not that it mattered. Colton's appetite wouldn't be any better than hers.

Colton sank onto the couch and put his face in his hands. "I should have stayed in Murphy. I could have invited you there."

She rested a palm on his knee. "Don't blame yourself. Hindsight's twenty-twenty. We both thought that once Perez's brothers were captured, you were safe. Everybody did."

He lowered his hands and looked at her. Moisture pooled against his lower lashes. "What am I going to do if they don't find him? I can't lose him, Jasmine."

Her heart twisted at the grief in his eyes. She wrapped both arms around him and squeezed, her face pressed to the side of his head.

Maybe her actions weren't professional. But this was what Colton needed. Besides, she wasn't his bodyguard anymore. The assignment was over. Now she was acting solely in the capacity of a friend.

When his arms circled her waist, the action silenced all her doubts. He held on to her in the same desperate way a drowning man clings to a life ring.

"They're going to find him." His breath was warm against the side of her neck. His tone held more hope than confidence.

She dropped her arms from around him and gripped his hands. "The guys who took him had to have a reason. When we find out what it is, we'll know better how to proceed."

"I can't imagine someone is holding him for ransom. There are lots of kids easier to get to than Liam and plenty of dads with more money than I have."

Colton was right. Finding a ransom note in the morning would be an easy resolution. But that wasn't likely to happen.

He drew in a deep breath. "The authorities are doing everything they can to find him. In the meantime, I'm trusting God to protect him. I've been praying for that since the moment I woke up."

The confidence she'd looked for earlier crept into his tone. He seemed sure prayer could make a difference.

But would God really hear him, one man among millions? What if God was busy elsewhere, doing important things, like preventing massive natural disasters or keeping the planets in their orbits?

Or maybe God did hear him, but instead of deliverance, this was one of those storms he was supposed to go through.

She tightened her fingers over his. No, she wasn't going to allow thoughts like that to stay in her mind. After losing his wife, Colton couldn't lose his son, too.

If only she'd been there. The score would have been more even—two against two. The thirty-eight at her hip would have made it even more so. Depending on how long Colton had been out, she might have missed the kidnapping by only ten or fifteen minutes.

The amount of time she'd taken to finish the last wall. The realization was like a steel-toed boot to the gut.

If she had stuck to the original plan and gotten to Colton's at three, Liam would possibly still be home. She closed her eyes and said a prayer of her own.

God, I don't have any reason to expect You to listen to me. But I'm begging You, for Colton's sake, please bring Liam back home.

Her prayers wouldn't hold any special power. She'd ignored God all her life.

But maybe, when combined with Colton's, they could have the ability to move the hand of God.

TEN

The jangling of the phone sent Colton's pulse into overdrive.

He pulled his hands from Jasmine's and rose. "My landline number is unlisted. I only have it to monitor the alarm."

He reached the kitchen at a half jog. Before snatching the receiver from the wall, he glanced at the caller ID. Blocked number displayed on the small screen, sending his tension skyrocketing. He pressed the phone to his ear and gave a breathless "Hello."

"You're not answering your cell phone."

The voice was gruff. Definitely not a friendly call. He glanced over his shoulder at Jasmine, who'd followed him into the kitchen. If he could keep the caller on the line long enough, maybe Jasmine could have the call traced.

He pulled a pen and sheet of paper from a drawer. "It didn't ring."

While he jotted down his phone number, the caller continued. "You thought you'd get away with it, didn't you?"

Get away with what? Making sure another criminal paid for his crimes?

He handed the paper to Jasmine. She was a step ahead of him and already had her cell phone in hand.

"Who is this?"

"You know who I'm calling for."

"Perez." The name slipped out before he could stop it.

The man laughed, the sound hard and cruel. "You've got so many people after you, you can't keep them straight."

Jasmine's soft voice came from the living room. She was probably on the phone with police. He needed to keep the caller on the line.

"Tell me what you want." Whatever it was, he'd find a way to give it to him. Anything to get his son back.

"I'm through waiting. Return what you took, or the boy dies."

His brain shut down. The man's last three words branded themselves on his mind. He was threatening to kill Liam.

Several moments passed before the first part of the sentence even registered. Return what he'd taken?

"What are you talking about?" This couldn't be connected with his job. Those decisions were irreversible, at least by him.

"I'll text instructions tomorrow morning. Make sure your phone is charged and working. If you don't show up at the appointed place and time with what you took in hand, the boy dies."

Panic pounded up his spine, scrambling his thoughts. How was he supposed to return something he didn't have? "I didn't take anything."

"If you want to see the boy alive, you'll follow my instructions explicitly. Don't involve the police or anyone else."

"Tell me what you want." His voice was several decibels louder than normal. But it didn't do any good, because he was talking to dead air.

He stared at the phone for several moments before placing it back on the hook. When he walked into the living room, Jasmine was pacing silently, phone still pressed to her ear. Her eyes met his, and he shook his head.

Her shoulders dropped. "He's gone. Were you able to get anything?" After a short pause, she disconnected the call. "The kidnappers?"

He nodded.

"Did they make a ransom demand?"

"They said if I don't return what I took, Liam dies."

"What did you take?"

"Nothing." He flung his arms wide, all the fear and frustration coming out in his tone. "How am I supposed to give them something when I have no idea what it is?"

"How long do you have?"

"I don't know. He's texting further instructions in the morning."

To his cell phone.

He charged into the kitchen and swiped it from the counter. "When I first picked up the call, he chided me for not answering my cell phone. I told him it didn't ring."

He checked his log. The last call was from Jasmine. Maybe it went straight to voice mail. He didn't know how, since he had full signal strength. After all, this was Atlanta, not rural Smoky Mountains.

But that explanation was better than the alternative, that the kidnappers had the wrong number and he wouldn't even get the text.

While he waited for his voice mail to connect, worry, fear and hopelessness melded into one toxic concoction. Moments later, a computerized voice said the words he dreaded—*You have no messages.*

Okay, maybe the kidnapper hung up when the call went to voice mail instead of leaving a message. He laid his phone back on the counter and squeezed his eyes shut. He was grasping at straws.

"The kidnappers have the wrong number. He hung up without giving me a chance to check it."

Jasmine put a hand on his arm, and he opened his eyes.

"When you don't respond to the text, he's going to figure it out. He'll call you on the landline again. And when he does, we need to be ready. Call the police. I'm calling Gunn."

She swiped her screen and pulled up her contacts.

"No." He covered her phone with his hand. "I can't involve anyone else. If I do, they'll kill Liam."

Her brows dipped toward her nose. "If you try to handle this alone, you could get both you and your son killed."

"But if they find out that I've involved the police or anyone from Burch Security, Liam is as good as dead. That's a chance I'm not willing to take."

She heaved a sigh, indecision flashing in her eyes. "Let me call Gunn, at least get his input. There might be a way to give you and Liam some security without the kidnappers finding out."

Colton stalked into the living room, unable to remain still. He didn't like it at all. The kidnapper had made himself clear—no one except Colton.

But bringing in other minds might be a good thing. "Advice only, right?"

"Yes. Tomorrow when he calls back, we'll figure out how to proceed. The final decision will be yours."

Colton's cell ringtone sounded from the kitchen, and his breath caught in his throat. For a split second, he stood frozen, then ran from the room, Jasmine right behind him. When he swiped his phone from the counter, Cade's name and number displayed on the screen.

His heart fell, and he gave his brother a weary "Hello."

Cade apparently didn't notice the heaviness in his voice. He didn't even try to temper that characteristic playfulness. "If you're spending Christmas with your hot new neighbor, I don't want to interrupt anything. But I did want to wish my favorite brother and nephew a merry Christmas."

Colton winced. The mention of Liam was like a red-hot poker through his heart.

"You can't talk to Liam. They took him." His tone was flat, in spite of the maelstrom of emotion swirling inside. If he didn't keep tight reins on it, he'd fall apart and never be able to pull himself back together.

"Who took him?"

"I don't know. The same guys as before."

"They found you in Murphy?"

"No, I'm in Atlanta." His gaze met Jasmine's. The sympathy and support he saw there bolstered him.

"What?" Cade's voice was almost shrill. "I told you not to come back to Atlanta."

"It was supposed to be safe. The authorities caught Perez's guys."

"These aren't Perez's guys." Cade screamed so loudly Colton held the phone away from his ear. "I told you to stay in Murphy."

He matched his brother's tone. "And I assured you I wasn't going anywhere until the people after us had been caught. They were caught last Thursday."

There was a muffled thud, like a boot hitting a wall. Or a fist. Cade wasn't just sick with worry. He was furious. He blew out a breath. "Has anyone made contact with you?"

"Someone called my landline and said if I don't return what I took, Liam dies."

"Oh, no. Oh, no. Oh, no." Cade released a long moan.

Colton's gut tightened. His brother's reaction didn't make him feel any better. Cade knew something. He'd said these weren't Perez's guys. Did he know who they were?

"Is there something you're not telling me?"

The pause that followed stretched out so long Colton thought the call dropped. "Cade?"

"I'm here." He released a long sigh. "I acquired a collection for a buyer, five Roman signet rings, circa second century. One was gold and oval-shaped eye agate, a beautiful piece. The agate was cone-shaped, with three color layers and an inscription on the face."

Colton curled his free hand into a fist. "Get to the point."

"It was exactly what I'd been searching for, for another buyer." After a brief pause, the rest of the words tumbled out. "I pulled it from the collection and replaced it with a fake."

Colton closed his eyes, clutching the counter for support. Cade had made some poor decisions in his life. But Colton had never known him to do something this stupid. "What were you thinking?"

"It was one piece out of five. And the fake was such high quality, *I* almost couldn't tell. I didn't think anyone would notice."

He clenched his teeth. If his brother were standing in front of him, Colton would have his fingers around his throat.

"Why did they go after Liam? I have nothing to do with the antiquities business."

"It's a case of mistaken identity."

Colton shook his head. That didn't explain anything. "How? I'm never at your business. It's on the opposite side of Atlanta from where I live and nowhere near where I used to work. Other than the fact that we look alike, there's nothing to lead them to me."

"While I was living at your house, I had some of my meetings there instead of in my office. It was more comfortable. We could kick back, have drinks, socialize. Your place is good for that, makes a good impression. Classy without being ostentatious."

Jasmine put a hand on his shoulder and squeezed. He needed it. He was probably growing paler by the second. The only thing keeping him on his feet was anger with his brother.

Cade continued. "They disabled the alarm at the business and ransacked it the night before coming to your place. I didn't learn that until later. When they didn't find the ring there, they came to the house."

The pieces of the puzzle were falling into place. And they weren't forming a pretty picture. Their father had made a good living dealing in antiquities. But that hadn't been enough for Cade. He'd wanted more. And he'd resorted to dishonesty to get it.

This probably hadn't been the first time he'd done something like this. He'd apparently had the connections in place when the need to quickly create a quality fake had presented itself.

Whatever stupid choices Cade made were his business. But how could he even think about pulling anything shady with people he'd brought into Colton's home? But that was just it. Cade didn't think. That had always been his MO—acting without weighing the consequences.

Colton pursed his lips. Cade had created the problem,

and Cade would have to fix it. Colton was not going to lose his son to his brother's greed.

"You have to get the original back from the other customer. Buy it back. Pay double if you have to."

"I can't. It disappeared from your house the day they tried to take Liam."

"What was it doing at *my* house?"

"I had it in my pocket in a small cloth bag when I stopped to see you and Liam the day before. I was meeting the other customer at his hotel room the following afternoon. Since I'd be running around with you in the morning and had the other appointment in the middle of the day, I took it out of the safe to bring home with me. I figured I'd save time backtracking to the south side of the city."

"And you stashed it at my house in the meantime."

"Not intentionally. Remember, I ended up having dinner with you, then staying the night. When Liam spilled his juice on me and you loaned me your sweats, I needed to put it somewhere safe."

"And why didn't you take it with you when you left?"

"Would you want to carry around a $20,000 artifact while running errands? I figured I'd pick it up when we got home, but I had to leave for my appointment right away. When I came back to get it, that's when I found out you'd been robbed, and it was gone."

"If they took it, why are they demanding I return it?"

"Maybe the guy that wants it doesn't know that."

"The guy you ripped off." His tone was heavy with disdain.

"The buyer. Maybe his goons decided to pick up some quick cash and pawn it themselves, then told him they couldn't recover it." Cade heaved another sigh. "I tried to make it right. I figured if I could get a similar piece, the problem would go away. I've made dozens of phone calls. I've got dealers all over the world searching. But until I had it in hand, I knew I didn't dare come back. And you couldn't, either."

"But you didn't bother to tell me."

"I did. I told you to stay away from Atlanta."

"But you didn't tell me why. You let me think all this time that Liam's attempted kidnapping had to do with one of my defendants."

"You were supposed to stay—"

"Don't try to place any of the blame for this on me." His angry outburst shut his brother up instantly. "If anything happens to Liam, I'll—"

He'd what? There was nothing he could do. Even if he never spoke to his brother again, it wouldn't bring his son back.

Rustling came through the phone. "I'm packing up now. I'll be at your place before morning."

"Where are you?"

"Grand Cayman. I'm catching the first flight out. I'll charter one if I have to."

"There's nothing you can do."

"There is. Marino tried to call me a half hour ago. I'm waiting to hear back from one other dealer. I wanted to have that answer before I took Marino's call."

Cade's cell phone. That was the number the kidnapper had. The phone where he'd text instructions tomorrow morning.

But he'd called Colton's landline. "How did he get the number to my house phone?"

"I made a few calls from it when my cell battery was low."

Colton closed his eyes again. His home and his phone.

Cade hadn't used Colton's name, but with their identical looks, he'd inadvertently impersonated him.

"I'll make this right." The urgency in Cade's voice pulled Colton's thoughts back to the conversation. "If I have to trade my own life for Liam's, I'll do it. If I'd had the piece, I'd have given it back immediately. I should have hidden it better."

No, he shouldn't have ripped anyone off to begin with. And he certainly shouldn't have involved his family.

"A jewelry box is the first place a thief looks for valuables."

Cade's words seemed to be an afterthought. But they slammed into Colton with the force of a freight train.

"Jewelry box?"

"Your closet door was open partway. When I was looking for a safe place to temporarily stash the piece, I saw Mandy's jewelry box on your shelf and dropped it into there."

Colton's heart beat so hard his chest felt ready to explode. "The intruders didn't empty the jewelry box. I did."

"What?" The single word held shock infused with hope.

"Remember the boxes I loaded into the back of the SUV before heading to the bank?"

"Mandy's clothes and things you were donating."

"I'd also transferred her jewelry to a zippered plastic bag and taken it with me, planning to put it in my safety deposit box while we were out. I ran out of time but stopped by both the ministry and the bank on my way to Burch Security the next day."

"The piece is in your safety deposit box?" Amazement filled his tone. A door slammed in the background.

"I'm going to find a flight out of here. As soon as I land, I'll call you. Then I'll take a cab straight to your place."

Colton ended the call, ready to fill Jasmine in on everything he'd learned. He was still almost frantic. But now a wide river of hope flowed through the worry that had almost debilitated him.

Cade's motto had always been "Nothing's going to happen." It was how he lived his life. Now Liam was taking the brunt of those bad decisions. But come tomorrow, Colton would be at the bank the moment the doors opened and he'd retrieve what Cade had stolen. Then he'd meet Liam's kidnappers. He'd give them the piece and they'd return Liam to him.

Unless something spooked them.

Or they decided to take revenge on Cade for what he'd done.

God, please make everything go as planned.

And protect Liam until he's back safe in my care.

Jasmine sat in the front passenger seat of Gunn's Range Rover. Black with tinted windows, it looked like something that might be used for surveillance. Currently, they were waiting in the shade of an oak at the far end of the bank parking lot, Gunn behind the wheel, Dom in the back. Her Suburban was parked two spaces away.

Convincing Colton to let the two men come had taken some effort. What part he'd allow them to play still remained to be seen.

Colton was inside the bank. So was Cade. Cade had driven his Corvette, while Colton had taken his own vehicle. Jasmine had followed at a distance to make sure they didn't pick up a tail. When they arrived, Dom and Gunn were already there.

Although they'd tossed around ideas and run through

scenarios, no one knew for sure what any of them would be doing. They couldn't formulate a plan until they heard from the kidnappers.

Gunn had pulled in some support, unbeknownst to Colton. He'd never have approved it. But they'd made other preparations, measures that Colton *did* approve. Cade's phone now had a tracker. Dom had installed the app. They'd also hidden a small tracking device inside the Corvette's dashboard.

From the moment the car left the bank parking lot, Dom would be viewing both the phone's and the car's movements on the laptop in the seat next to him. But the argument over who would meet the kidnappers was unresolved.

She'd rather it be her, or even Gunn or Dom. Any one of them would have a chance of finagling their way out of the situation. But Cade was too impulsive, and Colton, though good with persuasive words, had too much at stake to think clearly. Neither of them would know what to do if things went seriously south.

The bank's glass doors swung open, and Jasmine straightened. "Here they come."

At that distance, she couldn't tell them apart. Actually, she couldn't up close, either. They'd both dressed in blue jeans and black button-up shirts, if for nothing more than to create a moment of confusion should the opportunity present itself.

As the two men approached the passenger side of the Range Rover, Gunn turned the key and lowered the window. Jasmine studied them. The one on the right was Colton.

Maybe. The depth and seriousness she usually saw in Colton was present in both of them. The situation weighed on Cade enough that the carefree air he always projected was gone.

They moved between her and Gunn's vehicles, and one of them nodded at her. "We got it. Now we wait for the text."

Definitely Colton. She'd been right. His voice had a slightly different timbre from Cade's.

Cade frowned. "You need to give me the ring."

"No, *you* give *me* the phone."

"We talked about this at the house. I have to do this. It's bad enough I got you guys into this. If something happened to you, I'd never forgive myself."

"He's my son, so I'm going. If anything bad happens, you'll have to live with it." Colton's voice held a hardness she'd never heard before. This was likely to put a long-lasting wedge in his and Cade's relationship. If Colton lost Liam, that wedge would become a chasm, forever uncrossable.

"He's your son, but he's my nephew. And I'm the sole reason his life's in danger right now." Cade flung his arms wide, his whole body radiating his worry and frustration. "You go in and you could get yourself killed. You're not law enforcement. You don't know self-defense. The only fighting you've done is in the courtroom."

"And the only fighting you've done is on a mat in high school wrestling. You aren't any more qualified for this than I am."

Gunn let out a sharp whistle, making a *T* with his hands. "Time-out."

Everyone's attention went to him, and he continued.

"I don't like the idea of either of you doing this, but we don't have a choice. Colton is the boy's father, so it's his decision."

Cade looked ready to argue, but a text notification silenced him. His eyebrows shot up and he reached into his pocket. When he pulled out his phone, the screen was lit with recent activity.

Colton stepped closer, and his jaw tightened as he read. When he looked up, a vein throbbed in his temple.

"I'm to meet them at 148 Auburn Avenue with the ring. They reiterated that I'm to come alone. If they even *think* I've involved anyone else, Liam's dead." A steely hardness entered his eyes and he held out a hand, palm up. "Keys."

Cade pulled them from his pocket and turned them over. But he clearly wasn't happy. When Colton handed over his own keys, Cade took them with a frown.

"Don't try to follow me." Colton's tone was stern, discouraging any argument. "You can meet me back at the house later."

Jasmine's chest tightened. It was time. She stepped from the Range Rover with a lump in her throat and a sudden urge to wrap him in a tight hug.

She restrained the urge and simply took his hands in hers. "Be careful. Just focus on getting your son back. No heroics. Leave taking out the bad guys to the professionals."

He gave a sharp nod. He didn't seem the type to do anything stupid. He was levelheaded to the extreme.

But people sometimes lost capacity for rational thought when their loved ones were threatened. Restraining that need for vengeance wasn't easy. Colton especially would want the kidnappers to pay for their crimes. If he didn't have a strong sense of justice, he'd have chosen a different career.

Colton pulled his hands free of hers and pressed the fob. A corresponding beep sounded several spaces away, and the Vette's lights flashed. After sliding Cade's phone into his pocket, his gaze locked with hers.

"I'll call you when Liam and I are safe. Until then, I don't want you within a mile of the place. At this point, I don't even care if these guys are caught. I know I won't feel that way when it's over, but right now, I just want my son back."

"You should be wearing a wire, or at least a tracker."

"No." They'd discussed it last night, and he was as adamant now as he'd been then.

She touched her earpiece. No matter what happened, she'd have radio contact with Gunn and Dom. "We could conceal it."

"Unless it was something I could swallow, I'm not willing to take a chance."

Arguing with him was pointless, but she had to give it one last shot. "If they make you get in their vehicle and ditch your phone, we've lost you."

"Come on, Jasmine." The tension in his tone said he didn't like it any more than she did. "You heard the text. These guys don't play around. If they even *think* I'm pulling something, they're going to kill Liam. What do you think they'd do if they found a wire or tracking device on me?"

As he walked toward his brother's Corvette, a vise clamped down on her chest. But Colton wasn't alone in this, whether he wanted to be or not.

As soon as he'd relayed the location given in the text, she'd heard the click of the computer keys from the back seat. Even now, Dom was probably staring at a satellite image of the area, searching for a way to approach unseen.

But even with backup, there were a hundred things

that could go wrong, snafus that could get Liam or his father killed.

She drew in a stabilizing breath. She'd do anything to protect her clients. But Colton had become more than that. He'd even become more than a friend. She watched him back from the space, feeling as if someone was ripping her heart from her chest.

She reined in her thoughts. She had a job to do and was already at an extreme disadvantage. She needed to keep a clear head and be in top form, which meant operating like a machine—no emotion.

As Colton drove from the lot, she leaned down to look through the passenger window at Gunn. He already had the address programmed into the vehicle's GPS. She tilted her head. "What's the plan?"

He had to have one. He always did. So did Dom. She'd worked enough jobs with both of them to know.

"We follow. Stay out of sight. Assess when we arrive. See how close we can get without jeopardizing the safety of Colton or his son."

Beyond her boss, Cade had almost reached the Highlander three spaces away.

She straightened. "Hey." Her voice stopped Cade in his tracks. After waiting for him to turn, she continued. "You're with me."

Cade unleashed would be more of a liability than they could afford. As determined as he'd been to play the hero, she wouldn't put it past him to do something reckless.

Gunn cranked the engine. As she walked toward her own vehicle, she tilted her head toward Cade. "In the back."

"Why?"

"If you have to hit the floorboard, you can. Hiding is easier than in the front."

The explanation seemed to satisfy him. Which was good. Considering he was the sole reason they were there, if he decided to be argumentative, she might brain him.

She programmed the address into her own GPS and backed from the space. By the time she pulled into traffic, Gunn was several vehicles ahead of her. Colton would be too far away for even Gunn to see.

She slipped between two cars in the center lane, hoping to close the distance. "So where are we going?"

When Cade started to answer, she motioned toward her earpiece, and he fell silent. Dom's voice flowed through the wire, sounding as if he was much closer than several vehicles away. "148 Auburn Avenue is the old office of the Atlanta Life Insurance Company. The building's been vacant for decades."

"Is there a back way in?"

"I don't know. John Calhoun Park is right across Piedmont, which runs along the side of the building. Might be able to see something from there. Can't park there, though."

Jasmine changed lanes again. Now there were only two vehicles between them.

"I'll have a better chance of slipping in undetected than either of you." Besides, Colton was *her* client.

A few minutes later, she followed Gunn and another vehicle up the ramp onto I-85 South. The Corvette was still out of sight. If everything went smoothly, either she or Gunn would pass by the abandoned building early enough to see Colton exit the vehicle but late enough to avoid arousing suspicion. Everything else they were going to have to play by ear.

Not the way she preferred to operate.

After taking the John Wesley Dobbs exit, one more turn put them on Auburn, a single vehicle between them.

According to the GPS, they were less than a quarter mile from their destination.

The radio came to life again. "That's it, up ahead on the right."

Cade's Corvette was parked in the lot next to the building. Three stories, with neoclassical architecture, it had probably been pretty impressive in its day. But time had taken a toll. The brick was dingy; plywood covered the arched window openings and chunks of plaster were missing on some of the pillars.

"They're up ahead." It was Gunn who spotted them.

She saw them almost immediately also—two men moving down the sidewalk away from her, Colton on the right. The man next to him looked to be the same height but probably outweighed him by seventy-five pounds. They'd almost reached the next crossroad.

She chewed her lower lip. "Where is he taking Colton?"

Gunn didn't answer. She didn't expect him to. And Cade was being exceptionally quiet. The man walking with Colton swiveled his head slowly, glancing over his shoulder. His gaze seemed to lock on the Range Rover, but she couldn't see his eyes. He wore a cap pulled low, casting his face in shadow. If he was armed, his weapon was likely hidden under his lightweight jacket.

He wouldn't need it. Colton was no threat. As long as they held his son, he'd do exactly as instructed.

"Go around the block," she said. "I'm pulling over." Eight or ten parallel parking spaces bordered the edge of Auburn, starting just ahead of her and stretching almost to where Courtland crossed. "I'm following on foot."

"Don't let them see you." Gunn's tone held a note of warning.

She didn't need it. Having Colton spot her would be

just as dangerous as the kidnapper discovering her. He'd never be able to hide his reaction.

She cast a glance in the rearview mirror, peering at Cade through her sunglasses. "Get down."

Cade complied immediately. She slowed to a crawl and maneuvered into an empty space as Colton and his escort crossed the side street. Instead of continuing on Auburn, they turned right.

"They're headed north on Courtland now."

Jasmine looked around her. A modern building sat to her right—Georgia State University, Centennial Hall. Though she was five or six years past college age, she could probably blend in. Except the day after Christmas, the area was deserted.

She waited until Colton and the other man had disappeared around the side of the building, then opened her driver door. "I've got quarters in the console. Give it a minute, and if the coast is clear, feed the meter. Then get back in the vehicle."

Instead of staying on the sidewalk, she climbed the handful of stairs leading to Centennial Hall, then followed the perimeter of the building. Colton walked thirty or forty feet ahead of her on the opposite side of the street. The man with him regularly peered over his shoulder, scanning his surroundings.

For a short distance, she was able to keep to the school grounds until a fenced parking area stretched in front of her, giving her no choice but to follow the sidewalk. Trees lined her side of the road, but they weren't large enough to hide behind. And the five lanes of traffic moving toward her down the one-way street was sparse.

She slowed, letting the distance between her and the men lengthen, and pulled out her phone. With her head down, she slid her thumbs over the screen. If the man noticed her, he'd assume she was a student who didn't go home for the holidays. Colton hadn't turned around since she first saw him on Auburn. They'd almost reached the next crossroad when they changed direction.

"There's a parking lot on the west side of Courtland. They just walked into there." She stopped to lean against a tree. Her face was still tilted downward, but behind the sunglasses, her eyes shifted between her phone and where the men had gone.

"I don't like this." Gunn's tone was laced with concern.

A single beep sounded, and lights flashed on a red sports car. Her pulse kicked into high gear. The Atlanta Life Insurance Company wasn't the destination. The men had Liam somewhere else. And since Colton wasn't going there in Cade's Corvette, the tracking device would be worthless. They'd have to rely on what Dom had installed on the phone.

After a hand motion from the other man, Colton moved to the driver's side.

"They're getting into a vehicle, and Colton's driving."

"What kind of vehicle?"

"A red sports car. I'll give you the make in a minute. Where are you?"

"Three or four blocks away, on John Wesley Dobbs."

The engine turned over, and Colton backed from the space. Just before he made his right turn onto Courtland Street, the passenger window lowered. An object arced through the opening and landed on the sidewalk.

"The passenger just threw something out of the car."

"What?"

"I don't know yet."

Colton stepped on the gas and made his turn into the far-right lane. As the car approached, the man's gaze landed on her for the briefest moment before he looked away, apparently confident she didn't pose a threat. Colton stared straight ahead.

When they passed, she turned. Another vehicle overtook it, blocking her view. "I think it's a Mazda Miata, newer model. I couldn't get the tag."

She resumed walking again.

"See what he threw," Gunn said.

"Headed that way now."

She glanced over her shoulder. The Miata was making a left turn onto Auburn. Moments later, it was out of sight. As she drew closer to the parking lot, she picked up her pace, heart pounding. "Dom, are you showing movement on Cade's phone?"

What lay on the asphalt looked an awful lot like a cell phone.

Which meant the Miata was moving away with Colton inside. And no way to track him.

Time to call in some of those connections Gunn had put on standby. And hope that circumstances didn't throw them any other curveballs.

At least ones they weren't prepared to handle.

ELEVEN

Colton made his way east on Auburn, hands moist against the steering wheel.

The man in the passenger seat pressed his phone to his ear. "I've got him. We're headed your way."

Just like that, the conversation was over. He touched the screen and dropped the phone into his lap.

When Colton had arrived fifteen minutes ago, the parking lot next to the vacant building was empty. It wasn't until he got out and approached the door that the man stepped around the corner and led him to the other side of the building.

Moments later, he was thanking the Lord that he hadn't allowed any of the Burch Security people to fit him with a wire or tracking device. In the small space between that building and the next, the guy frisked him so thoroughly he would have found it. He even made him take off his shoes and empty his pockets.

The precautions hadn't ended there. When they'd reached the car, the man had demanded he hand over his cell phone. He'd spent the next minute scrolling through calls and texts.

And Colton had sweated bullets the entire time. He had no clue what was there. It wasn't his phone.

Apparently, nothing had set off alarms. The only thing the man had wanted to know was who he'd talked to last night. Colton had said he'd wished his brother a merry Christmas.

He hadn't, but Cade had. Since he was playing the part of Cade, what he'd said was true. The man had seemed satisfied with the explanation.

Then he'd thrown the phone out the window.

"Turn right up here." The command cut into Colton's thoughts.

He signaled, looking at the street sign as he approached. Boulevard. He knew the area. He knew most of Atlanta. But he had no idea where the man was taking him.

The Burch Security people wouldn't, either. Neither the tracking device in Cade's car nor the app installed on Cade's phone were going to do him any good. Whatever happened, he'd be facing it alone.

No, he wasn't alone. He needed to keep reminding himself of that. He was never alone.

God, please protect Liam and be with me. Help me get him back and please don't let either of us get hurt.

He braked leading up to the turn, then accelerated as he straightened the wheel. Sporty and low to the ground, the car handled well. Under other circumstances, he'd enjoy the snazzy ride. Now he just wanted to get to wherever they were holding Liam.

The man directed him through a couple more turns until he was traveling east on Dekalb Avenue. A low rumble sounded in the distance, somewhere behind them.

Colton checked the rearview mirror. A box truck occupied the majority of the rectangular space.

He shifted his gaze to the side mirror. In the upper part

of the glass, a helicopter hovered against a partly cloudy sky. It seemed to be flying lower than normal.

His heart pounded as an odd mixture of hope and dread swirled inside him. Jasmine and her partners had wanted to implement more security measures, and he hadn't let them.

Maybe they'd moved ahead with their plans anyway. If so, there would be professionals on his side.

And all kinds of things that could go wrong. The men had warned him—if he involved anyone else, Liam would die.

He slid a nervous glance toward the man next to him. He'd noticed the helicopter, too. He sat staring at his own side mirror, tension radiating from him.

He picked up his phone and touched the screen. "We might have company. There's a chopper headed right toward us."

In the pause that followed, he kept his gaze fixed on the side mirror. "Don't worry, we're not coming to you till I know it's clear."

He slid Colton a sideways glance. "I don't think he's that stupid. He knows we mean business."

He dropped the phone back into his lap. "I'm right, aren't I? You didn't do anything stupid like calling the police?"

"Of course not." Actually, that wasn't true. "I called them when it first happened, but that was before you made contact. They know nothing of this meeting."

He struggled to keep the nervousness from his voice. He didn't have anything to hide. He wasn't the one who summoned that chopper. Maybe no one had.

He watched it until it disappeared from view, now too high to be visible in the mirror. The rumble increased in volume until it seemed to come from all around them.

The man removed a weapon from beneath his jacket and pointed it at him. "If you've pulled something, the boy won't be the only one who dies. You're going to join him."

"I'm not pulling anything." The panic ricocheting through him made the words come out louder than he intended. "I didn't call anyone."

He leaned toward the window and cast a quick glance over his left shoulder. The chopper was gaining on them, poised to pass almost over them.

He released a sudden sigh of relief. "That's not the police." He should have thought of it sooner. "Atlanta's choppers are black."

That one was white. As it moved past them, he read the letters painted on the side and bottom.

"It's from one of the local news stations. They might even be doing traffic."

The man seemed to relax. Colton almost crumpled. One disaster averted. The man was jittery. Likely, both kidnappers were.

Colton gripped the wheel more tightly. If he could get through the entire exchange with nothing spooking them, he and Liam might have a chance of surviving the day.

The chopper moved ahead, and the man pointed. "Take the next right."

Colton did as told. It looked like they were proceeding as planned. Since they didn't seem to be heading toward any of the large roads leading away from Atlanta, the meeting location was probably somewhere nearby.

When the man directed him through another turn, the sign at the corner triggered a vague sense of familiarity. Rogers Street. Why did it ring a bell?

He followed a ninety-degree curve and scanned his surroundings. The Circus Arts Institute stood on the right. On the left, a chain-link fence ran parallel to the road, barbed wire on top. Red no-trespassing signs were affixed at points along its length. Beyond, metal buildings were spread out over the landscape, towering, barn-like structures that obviously hadn't seen any activity in decades.

The Pullman train yard. Now he knew why the street name sounded familiar. He'd read a news piece about the place, that a film production company had purchased the long-abandoned complex with big plans to turn it into a mini city with a boutique hotel, restaurants and a public gathering space for movies and concerts.

But none of those improvements had begun. Even in broad daylight, an eerie air of abandonment hung over the property. Any one of those graffiti-covered buildings would be the perfect place for an exchange like this to go down.

"Pull over here."

Just ahead on the right was a cleared area, large enough for a vehicle to turn around. Beyond a chain-link fence, grassy fields were visible in a break between trees. A sign next to the locked gate announced Welcome to the Arizona Avenue Fields.

Colton pulled off the road and eased to a stop in front of the gate. Maybe someone would question the car being parked illegally and call the police.

Not likely. Since they were on Rogers rather than Arizona, the entrance he was blocking was likely a back way in.

Colton turned off the engine. The Miata was the only vehicle there. "Where is Liam?"

Instead of answering the question, the man spoke into his phone. "We're here...no, we weren't followed."

As he spoke, he wrapped a handkerchief around the

door handle and opened it. He'd done the same thing getting in, careful to not leave prints. Maybe he planned to ditch the car when everything was over. It was likely a rental, obtained with fake identification.

Colton stepped from the car. "Where are we going?" The gates to the train yard and the athletic fields were chained and padlocked.

The man didn't answer that question, either. "Open the trunk."

Colton did as instructed. It was empty except for some bolt cutters. So that was how they'd get inside the fence, likely the one across the street. He picked up the tool and held it out.

The man leaned against the car, then motioned toward the train yard. "You cut. I'll keep watch."

Yeah, he wasn't going to leave prints on the bolt cutters, either. Colton crossed the street and knelt on the narrow strip of grass in front of the fence. He'd completed several snips in a horizontal path when the man stopped him.

"Get over here. Someone's coming. Act like you're getting something out of the trunk."

Colton's stomach tightened. He didn't need a Good Samaritan stopping to lend a helping hand. Contact with anyone, even random strangers, could spook the men.

Leaving the cutters in the grass, he rose and walked toward the Miata. A white minivan moved toward them. A short distance behind it was an SUV.

Two for one. Good. The fewer interruptions he had, the sooner he'd see his son.

He leaned into the trunk, not straightening until the second vehicle had passed. When the road was clear again, he returned to his task. Soon the cuts formed a decent-sized upside-down *L* that ended at the ground.

When he turned for further instructions, the man was crossing the street.

"Crawl through."

Colton pushed on the cut section, forcing it inward. As he slipped through the opening, a sharp piece of fence grabbed his sleeve, ripping the fabric and scraping his shoulder. After a final glance in both directions, the man struggled to follow him inside. The opening was almost too small.

He got to his feet, and Colton followed him toward the graffiti-covered buildings. Every square foot of reachable surface showcased the creativity of local urban artists. Even though he didn't approve of defacing property, he had an appreciation for the talent displayed.

Instead of walking into the nearest building, the man led him past it. Ahead was a hodgepodge of brick-and-steel structures. Wide bay doors spanned the side of the nearest one.

Once sure of their destination, he picked up his pace. Liam was likely inside.

He stepped beneath one of the partially raised doors and scanned the huge open space. Metal framework supported a pitched roof probably thirty feet high at its center. Sunshine struggled in through dirt-streaked skylights. Graffiti decorated the lower portions of the walls and metal posts, and rainwater had pooled in places on the concrete floor.

A rustle of movement drew his attention, and he turned. It was just the man who'd brought him here.

"Where is Liam?" He fought to keep the panic from his voice. Someone was supposed to be there waiting with his son.

What if Liam wasn't there? What if the men had lured

him to the abandoned train yard with plans to kill him and take the ring?

God, please protect us both.

"Be patient. They're here." He crossed his arms and leaned against one of the metal support posts. The pose highlighted the size of his chest and biceps, even through the jacket. "But they're not going to show themselves until they know it's safe."

Colton's panic lessened, but not by much. He wouldn't relax until he and Liam were far away from here. For the past few weeks, wherever he'd gone, Jasmine had had his back. What he wouldn't give now to know she was somewhere close.

A sound set his pulse pounding. Did he hear a child's whimper? He froze, hope tumbling through him.

When he heard it again, he turned in that direction. Windows encrusted with decades of dirt lined the wall adjacent to where he'd entered. Trees stood a short distance beyond them.

A figure moved past. Then another. The silhouette of the first one was bulkier, as if the person was carrying something.

Like a small child.

Now he had no doubt. What he'd heard was a child's soft cry. The whimpering was closer now, filled with loneliness and despair.

A vise clamped down on his chest, squeezing the air from his lungs. When someone holding his son entered through one of the bay doors, his knees almost buckled.

Liam was safe. He was scared, but he appeared unhurt.

Colton took several stumbling steps forward. Now that Liam had seen him, his whimpers had escalated to wails. He was kicking and twisting, trying to get down, both arms stretched toward Colton.

"Hey."

The shout didn't register until too late. The larger man thrust out an arm, lightning fast. The back of his fist caught Colton in the stomach.

Colton skidded to a stop, doubled over at the waist. Liam screamed more loudly.

A third man entered. "Shut him up."

Colton straightened, his heart in his throat. "It's okay, buddy. Daddy's here." He shouted the words, but Liam seemed not to hear him. A good thirty feet separated them, and Liam was as distraught and terrified as he was after one of his nightmares.

The man holding him started to bounce him, and Colton continued.

"Don't cry, buddy. Daddy's going to take you home."

The screams settled into sobs, and Colton released a pent-up breath.

The last man who entered spoke. "You have what I told you to bring?"

Colton nodded. Since all his attention had been on his son, he hadn't given the man more than a passing glance.

Now he did. This was Marino. Even without the description Cade had given him early this morning, he'd have known. The other two seemed like enforcers, thugs who carried out the orders of others. Marino didn't.

He was bald, stocky and short—probably only five-six or five-seven. But he projected an aura of power. He was used to giving orders and having them obeyed.

"I have it." He removed the item from his pocket. "Take it, and let me have my son."

Marino stayed where he was. "Boulder, bring me the ring."

Boulder. Obviously a nickname, probably a reference to his size. Colton placed the small cloth bag into the man's extended hand. Boulder carried it to Marino without opening it.

"I have to make sure it's the real thing." Marino opened the bag, then nailed Colton with a cold glare. "Since the dealer has no integrity."

Colton felt an odd sense of shame that wasn't his to bear. He fought the urge to defend himself, to set the record straight.

But he had no defense. What Cade did was inexcusable. And all three men believed he was Cade.

"This is the original. I guarantee it." Not that Cade's promises meant anything.

Marino removed the ring from its protective bag. As he studied it, Colton fidgeted. What if the original was a fake? What if someone had slipped a reproduction into the collection before Cade acquired it?

No, Cade would have recognized it. He was too good at what he did.

Seconds stretched into a half minute. Everything was silent except for Liam's muffled sobs. And something a lot more distant. The squeal of sirens.

As the volume increased, Colton stopped breathing. Jasmine wouldn't have called the police. Even if she had, they wouldn't descend on the place with their sirens screaming. Atlanta PD was much better at stealth than that.

Colton studied the men. He wasn't the only one who was nervous. Boulder and the man holding Liam shifted from one foot to the other, their stance alert, as if ready for a quick exit. The only one unruffled by the approaching sirens was Marino.

Boulder drew his weapon. "Come on, let's dump the kid and get out of here."

"Not so fast." Marino walked slowly toward the other

side of the building, his dress shoes making rhythmic taps against the concrete. Halfway across, he turned to retrace his steps. Rather than to calm himself, the pacing seemed more for the purpose of putting others on edge.

"Mr. Gale here had his instructions." His speech was as lazy as his mannerisms. "If he chose to ignore those instructions, the kid will pay."

Colton gasped. "I didn't call anyone." As hard as he tried, he couldn't keep the quiver out of his voice. Or the desperation. "Those sirens have nothing to do with me."

Acres of overgrowth and abandoned steel-and-brick buildings gave the impression of complete solitude. But it was an illusion. The bustle of the city was only a few blocks away.

"This is Atlanta. You hear sirens twenty-four hours a day."

As emergency vehicles moved even closer, the lankier man placed Liam on the floor but kept a tight grip on his hand. He, too, drew his weapon.

The squeals reached their loudest, then started a slow fade. Judging from the direction and closeness of the sirens, they had likely passed by on Dekalb.

Colton drew in a shaky breath, every nerve frayed. "Come on, I've held up my end. I brought you what you wanted and I didn't involve anyone else. Let me have my son."

Marino stared at him, and a shiver skittered down Colton's spine. There was something about the set of the other man's jaw, the hardness that had entered his features. His eyes held coldness, even cruelty.

"Move to the other end of the building."

"What?"

"You heard me."

Colton hesitated, not wanting to put even more distance between him and his son. But he had no choice. Marino had all the power. He had none.

He walked, casting repeated glances backward. The building was long, probably close to three hundred feet from end to end.

"You made a promise." He flung the words over his left shoulder. "You said if your terms were met, you'd return my son unharmed."

When he reached the far end, he turned. Bay doors occupied the entire wall to his right. The three men were spread out in front of two of the doors near the opposite end.

His gaze shifted to the windows several hundred feet in front of him. Had he just seen movement? A brief silhouette of someone moving against the woods?

No, that was wishful thinking. No one was coming to rescue him.

He prayed he wouldn't need it. Maybe Marino had an innocent reason for sending him so far from his son. Maybe their plan was to release Liam to go to him while they ran from the building to whatever means of escape they had waiting.

It wouldn't be the Miata. He was sure of that. Otherwise Boulder wouldn't have been so careful about not leaving behind prints.

Marino gave a slight nod. "Let him go."

The man dropped Liam's hand. For several moments, Liam stood unmoving, eyes wide, thumb in his mouth.

"Come on, buddy." Colton held out both arms, relief and joy colliding inside him. It was almost over. Within a minute or two, he and Liam would walk from the building.

He had no phone, no way to get in touch with Jasmine and the others. But he'd find a way. He could walk to a nearby business. Or flag down a motorist.

Liam pulled his thumb from his mouth and began moving toward him, picking up speed as he went. Colton struggled to remain where he was. Marino had made him walk to the far end of the building and probably expected him to stay there.

But everything inside him demanded that he run to his son, scoop him up and disappear out the nearest door. Instead, he dropped to one knee and spread his arms wider.

Moments later, Liam tripped and crashed to the floor. He remained on his hands and knees as renewed sobs shook his little shoulders.

That protective instinct took over, and Colton shot to his feet. He'd covered about half the distance when Marino spoke, voice devoid of emotion. "Shoot the kid."

Colton's heart stuttered as he skidded to a stop. "What?"

Several seconds passed before he realized he'd heard his question in chorus. He wasn't the only one who'd voiced an objection. Boulder still held his weapon poised but was shaking his head.

"I said shoot the kid. Mr. Gale needs to learn there are consequences for trying to rip people off. Especially people like me."

Colton shifted his gaze to the windows, then immediately snapped it back again. Someone was out there.

Was it kids doing unauthorized exploration? Or trained people who were qualified to lend a hand? If the latter, was there any chance they'd get there in time?

The larger man lowered his weapon. "No way. I don't kill kids."

A figure bolted past the first opening. The bay door was raised only a couple of feet, but he recognized those boots.

Jasmine!

How had she found him? If she was there, that probably meant Gunn and Dom were there, too.

"You'll do as I say."

Colton's mind spun. He needed to give them time to get into position to stop the men before anyone opened fire.

"You've got what you want." He spoke with more boldness than he felt. "You need to leave while you can."

He hesitated, thoughts still swirling. "That helicopter we saw, they weren't just looking for news. They were tracking me."

Okay, that was pretty far-fetched. But it was the best he could come up with on the spur of the moment.

"I'm sure the authorities have already located the car and are moving in as we speak. If anyone fires a weapon, guys with guns are going to be all over this place."

Marino gave a derisive laugh. "You're full of it. Just like you were when you tried to pass off a fake Roman signet ring for a real one."

Marino's words were convincing, but a seed of doubt had crept in, tainting that air of confidence. If there was anything Colton had learned as a prosecutor over the years, it was how to read people.

"You don't know that for sure. Do you really want to stake your freedom on it? What if you're wrong?"

Two more figures slipped past the opening, likely Gunn and Dom.

Marino shifted his attention back to Boulder. "Now do what I said."

Colton held up a hand. "Wait." The three bodyguards were just outside, making their way closer along the side of the building. The next two doors were closed, the fourth being the first open enough to walk under without ducking. They needed a few more seconds to reach it.

Suddenly, another set of legs appeared in front of the first door. The next second, Cade dropped to the ground and rolled beneath it. A moment later, he was on his feet, creeping silently toward the three men.

What was he doing? He'd probably been instructed to stay in the vehicle. Instead, he was going to try to play the hero. It was a good way to get them all killed.

"No more stalling." Ice tinged Marino's tone. "Do it."

"I told you, I don't kill kids. I won't live with that on my conscience."

"No, I guess you won't." Marino reached beneath his jacket. In one smooth motion, he withdrew his weapon, aimed it and fired.

Boulder twisted and lunged, but not quickly enough to avoid the bullet. He clutched his side and dropped to his knees.

Cade charged Marino the same time Colton ran full bore toward his son. Liam had sat back on his heels and was screaming, eyes squeezed shut and hands pressed to his ears.

Marino brought the weapon around and pointed it at Liam.

The next several seconds played out in slow motion. Colton shot forward in a final burst of speed. Jasmine, Dom and Gunn ran through the open door, and Cade slammed into Marino.

Gunfire exploded a second time. Colton's leg buckled, and he crashed to the concrete. Pain ricocheted through his body, the keenest agony centered in his right thigh.

He covered the final few feet at a sloppy crawl while chaos erupted a few yards away. Another shot rang out. A quick glance that direction confirmed that neither Cade nor any of the Burch Security people had been hit.

He sat and scooped Liam into his lap. His pants leg

was soaked. He was losing blood fast. While he put pressure on the wound with one hand, he held Liam to his chest with the other, rocking him back and forth and whispering soothing words into his ear.

Sirens sounded in the distance, filling him with relief instead of fear. This time, they were probably for him.

He looked up to see both Marino and the thinner man lying on the floor facedown, their hands behind their heads. Gunn's and Dom's weapons were trained on them. Boulder was lying nearby with Cade kneeling over him trying to staunch the flow of blood. The man was still conscious, but just barely. He'd refused to kill Liam. Colton hoped he made it.

Jasmine had just risen and was walking toward him and Liam. Sunlight washed over her as she passed under one of the skylights.

Never had he seen anything so beautiful.

If not for her and the other Burch Security people, Liam would be dead. Colton likely would be, too. He owed her everything.

When she dropped to her knees in front of him, he wrapped his arms around her, Liam pressed between them. The next moment, his lips were on hers and he was pouring everything he felt into the kiss—respect, admiration, appreciation.

And love.

Love?

He stiffened. Mandy had been gone for just seven months. How could he even think about letting go of what he'd had with her and giving it to someone else?

He pulled away, letting his arms fall from around her. "I'm sorry. I was with my wife for seven years. I haven't even dated anyone since she died."

Jasmine brought a hand to her mouth. Her fingers

quivered, and her eyes held confusion. "It's okay. I'm not any more ready for this than you are." She looked down at his leg. "Are you all right?"

His leg. Yes. No. "I got shot."

She'd been quick to dismiss what had just happened between them. Good. It was for the best.

"I know how bad it hurts. I've been there." She gave him a weak smile. "Help is almost here."

The sirens were louder now, almost ear-piercing. They'd likely turned off Dekalb and were now on Rogers. Someone needed to tell them where they were.

Colton searched for Cade, but he was gone. Maybe he'd gone out to meet law enforcement and emergency medical personnel. Today he'd taken a small step toward atoning for his wrongs. But he still had a long way to go.

"Are you staying with me?" Jasmine's hands pushed his aside to press down on his leg, and he grimaced.

"Yeah." At least he was trying. His stomach threatened to hurl its contents and shadows danced on the edges of his vision.

He wasn't going to pass out. Not with Jasmine watching. If their roles were reversed and she was the one lying there with a bullet in her leg, she'd stoically bear both the pain and the blood loss. She was one tough lady. She'd served on the front lines in one of the scariest places on earth. And she'd been shot, probably more than once.

The shadows darkened. No, he was *not* going to pass out.

Keeping pressure on his leg with one hand, Jasmine reached for Liam with the other. "You'd better lie down. You're looking really pale."

"I'm all right." Beyond her, four police officers and two paramedics entered the building. He seemed to be watching them through a tube that was growing smaller by the second.

"You're not all right." She wrapped an arm around Liam and dragged him onto her lap.

Colton allowed her to gently push him backward. From this perspective, everything looked different, the ceiling a maze of metal trusses and beams, maybe even a couple of catwalks.

"Is anyone else hurt?" The male voice likely belonged to one of the paramedics. He couldn't look to see. The clouds had moved across his entire field of vision.

"Over here. Gunshot wound to the thigh." Jasmine sounded far away. But she was there. He could still feel the pressure of her hand on his leg.

He wasn't going to pass out, but someone would have to watch Liam during the ambulance ride and his time at the hospital.

Cade would gladly do it, but as far as Colton was concerned, he'd lost that privilege.

He reached for Jasmine. "Please take care of Liam."

She squeezed his hand. "Of course I will."

A sense of peace settled over him. His son was finally safe. It really was over.

Thank You, Lord.

He released a long sigh and gave in to the oblivion overtaking him.

TWELVE

Colton shifted his position and wasn't quite able to stifle a grimace.

Jasmine gave him a sympathetic smile. "Does it hurt bad?"

"Not as badly as I'd expect it to."

He probably had some heavy-duty pain meds to thank for that. He'd woken up in Recovery an hour ago and eventually been moved to a semiprivate room.

The other bed was empty, which was a good thing. It hadn't taken long for the room to fill with visitors. Jasmine, Gunn and Dom had come into the room within minutes of the nurses getting him settled in the bed.

His Murphy friends were lending their support, too. Jasmine had texted Paige, who'd relayed what had happened to Tanner, who'd passed the information on to Andi and Bryce. Tanner and Paige had walked in a few minutes ago. Andi and Bryce hadn't arrived yet but were on their way.

Jasmine had even been allowed to bring Liam into the room. He'd immediately wanted to climb up into the bed, and Colton had let him. For the past several minutes, Liam had lain with his head on Colton's shoulder, his arm stretched across his chest.

When the nurses eventually ran out all the visitors, Liam wasn't going to be happy. Colton wasn't, either. Liam would be in good hands with Jasmine, but after coming so close to losing him, Colton wanted to hold on to him forever.

He looked at Dom and Gunn, then let his gaze settle on Jasmine. "I need to tell you guys thanks for not listening to me. I don't even want to think about what would have happened if you hadn't gotten involved."

Jasmine shrugged. "That's what we do. What kind of bodyguard would I be if I let you meet kidnappers alone? I'm just glad it worked out."

His eyes shifted to the corner. His brother stood several feet away, back against the wall. He'd ridden there with Jasmine and Liam. But when the others had gathered around the hospital bed, Cade had hung back, face lined with fatigue and eyes projecting sadness.

Yeah, he blew it. And he knew it.

Colton winced as compassion tugged at him. He tamped it down. Cade had acted heroically in the end, but he didn't deserve to be welcomed back into their lives as if the events of the past twenty-four hours hadn't happened.

He pulled his attention back to Jasmine. He had a whole slew of unanswered questions. In the few minutes they'd been there, the conversation hadn't progressed beyond them asking how he felt and his checking on his son.

"How did you find us?"

"I guess you could say we know people in high places." She smiled. "None of us were comfortable with not being able to track you except through your phone and car. We knew we needed a plan B. So Gunn got ahold of a friend who covers traffic for one of the local news stations. He told her the situation, that we might need some help."

"The helicopter." Colton released a laugh. "When the men were going to shoot Liam, I said the helicopter had been tracking me. I was making something up, trying to convince them to take the ring and disappear."

"That was a pretty good guess. When I realized they'd ditched your phone, Gunn placed a call to someone at the station. His friend kept an eye on you until she knew where you were going."

He nodded. "Liam and I both owe our lives to you three."

Jasmine shrugged. "Everyone played a part."

Colton frowned. "I didn't do much."

"You did. It was your trying to persuade the guy to not shoot that bought us the time we needed."

Yeah, persuasive argument. That was his specialty. He wasn't good with a firearm, and he probably wouldn't fare well in hand-to-hand combat. But thinking on his feet? That was something he could do.

"Cade was supposed to wait in the car." She cast a quick glance over her shoulder. "But it's a good thing he didn't. He'd slipped up behind us, so we didn't even realize what he'd done until we rushed into the building."

She was right. Cade's actions had been reckless. But they'd saved Liam's life.

"Who fired the last shot?"

"The thinner guy. It was intended for Cade, but Dom tackled him first. Dressing alike had been a good idea."

Gunn nodded. "When the guy saw Cade, his mouth dropped open. He looked at you, then back at Cade. By the time he recovered enough to fire, Dom was taking him down. So the shot went wide."

God had allowed all the pieces to fall perfectly into place. The extra set of eyes in the sky, the Burch Security people arriving when they did, Cade's reckless but heroic actions, even the man refusing to shoot Liam.

"What about the bigger guy who got shot? How is he?"

Jasmine shrugged. "He was still alive at the time they took him away from the scene, but that's all I know."

"I hope he makes it."

She shook her head. "You and Liam almost died today. But you're concerned about the condition of one of the bad guys. Somehow that doesn't surprise me."

There was no criticism in her tone. Instead, her eyes held respect and admiration. She'd hinted at it before— she'd been observing him, watching how he lived out his faith, searching for the same peace he'd found.

But having a soft spot in his heart for the man who'd chosen to let his son live was easy. Letting go of the anger with his brother wasn't. He'd put Liam in grave danger, for nothing except greed.

Colton's gaze wandered again to the lone figure against the wall. Cade's eyes held a silent plea for forgiveness. That same nudge poked at him again, harder to ignore than before.

He curled his hand into a fist. He didn't want to make amends with his brother. Not right now. He wanted to nurse his anger a little longer.

Maybe Cade had learned his lesson. Maybe not. Frankly, it wasn't Colton's concern. What Cade had done was between him and God.

And whether Colton chose to forgive was between *him* and God. He knew what God required. Hating his brother or even remaining angry wasn't an option.

Andi and Bryce walked into the room and joined the other five gathered around the hospital bed.

Bryce clasped Colton's hand in a firm grip. "You'll

do anything for attention, won't you? But almost getting yourself killed is going too far."

Colton laughed. "I think I've had enough attention for a while. I'm looking forward to returning to Murphy for a quiet and uneventful life."

Gunn gave him a high five. "I'll second that. Here's to the hope that you'll never need our services again, and that all future interactions with Jasmine will be strictly personal."

Gunn and Dom made their farewells, but before they could leave, a nurse walked in. With her salt-and-pepper hair pulled into a tight bun and a stern set to her jaw, she looked like an old-time schoolteacher. The kind that carried a thick ruler.

"Looks like there's a party going on in here."

Andi stepped aside to allow her to approach the bed. In spite of the no-nonsense demeanor, her touch was gentle. She checked his temperature and made a notation in the chart.

"How are you feeling?"

"I've had better days, but I've also had worse." Like yesterday, when he hadn't known whether he was going to see his son again. He offered up another prayer of thanks.

When the nurse finished checking his vitals, she scanned the faces of his friends. "Mr. Gale just got shot. He needs his rest."

She was probably right. They'd told him he'd lost a lot of blood. Besides the pain medication, they had him on some heavy antibiotics and were keeping him overnight for observation.

The rest she'd ordered sounded good. Maybe it was the effects of the anesthesia. Or not sleeping in more than twenty-four hours. Or the fact he'd just gone through the scariest experience of his life. But exhaustion was quickly overtaking him.

Dom lifted a hand. "At least two of us are on our way out."

Jasmine reached for Liam. "And this little guy looks like he's ready for a nap."

Liam gave brief half-hearted resistance before wrapping his arms around Jasmine's neck. As she walked toward the door, Cade followed.

Colton's jaw tightened. He wasn't ready to welcome his brother back into his life, but he had to begin the healing process. "Cade?"

Cade turned. The hope in his eyes squeezed Colton's chest further.

"Thanks for what you did today."

"It was the least I could do."

"It was brave and selfless."

Maybe today's events *would* be a turning point for Cade. *Selfless* wasn't an adjective he'd ever expected to use to describe his brother.

Colton watched them walk away, then motioned toward his Murphy friends. "These guys just drove two hours to get here. I'll run them out when I get tired."

The nurse gave a sharp nod, then left the room.

Bryce moved closer. "So what happened? All Jasmine's text said was that Liam had been recovered and everyone was okay, but you'd been shot."

Colton relayed the entire story, starting with last night's phone call from the kidnappers.

When he'd finished, Andi shook her head. "That's scary. At least it's over."

Colton released a sigh. "Thank You, Lord."

"So what now?" Bryce asked.

"When I get out of here, Liam and I will head back to Murphy."

"What about Jasmine?"

"She'll move on to her next assignment."

"And that's it?"

Colton shrugged. "We've talked about staying in touch, for Liam's sake. Unfortunately, he's gotten attached to her."

Tanner cocked his head to the side. "What about you?"

Colton shifted position and pain ripped through his thigh. Whatever they'd given him in Recovery was starting to wear off.

But the wound wasn't his only discomfort. Tanner and Bryce were ganging up on him. And he knew where they were headed.

"We're friends. That's all."

Tanner frowned. "That's what you say, but it's not how you feel. And there's no sense trying to deny it. It's obvious every time you look at her."

"My focus is on my son. He comes first."

Bryce shook his head. "Doing what makes you happy and what's best for Liam aren't mutually exclusive."

He crossed his arms and glared at his friends. He was outnumbered. Though neither of the women had spoken, they'd nodded their agreement.

"Give me a break. I just got shot."

"Hey, turnabout's fair play."

He narrowed his eyes at Tanner. "What's that supposed to mean?"

"Remember when I was ready to let Paige walk out of my life? You were the one who talked some sense into me. I'm returning the favor."

"I don't need either of you meddling in my business."

Bryce held up both hands. "All right. We won't bother you anymore. At least until you get out of the hospital."

Great. They were giving him a reprieve, but it was only temporary.

He and Bryce had been friends since he was fifteen, he and Tanner longer than that. Those guys knew him better than his own parents did. But that didn't mean they had all the insight into his love life.

Bryce had said to think about it. He already had. There'd been that kiss, initiated during a time of extreme emotional stress. But they'd both agreed it was a mistake. Jasmine wasn't interested, and he didn't blame her. Why would she give up her freedom to take on the responsibility of another woman's child? And the thought of allowing someone else to take Mandy's place in his or Liam's life still tied his insides into knots.

His curt response had ended the conversation with his friends. But long after they left, their words still circled through his mind.

And each argument he posed seemed less and less convincing.

Jasmine turned onto Hilltop Road and released a sigh. Today started a new year. A year filled with uncertainty. Colton had insisted that she come up and join him and Liam for lunch. He'd said he needed to make up for the Christmas dinner that had never materialized.

Returning to the cozy house, even for a visit, was a bittersweet experience. She'd come here a month ago, ready for another typical assignment. She'd approached this one like she had all her others—with confidence and cool professionalism, emotionally detached.

No assignment was "just a job." Whether she was providing extra security for a visiting celebrity or protecting a woman from a crazed ex-boyfriend, she gave it her all, throwing herself into the line of fire to protect her charge from harm.

But she always kept a distinct line between her professional and her personal life. No, not a line—a chasm, a virtual Grand Canyon. Or a wall. The Great Wall of China.

Until this time. Somehow, one sad little boy and his grieving father had changed that.

Maybe it was all the times she'd rocked Liam, soothing away his fears after a terrifying nightmare. The way he'd snuggled against her and wrapped his arms around her waist. Those times he'd called her Mommy and melted her heart.

Maybe it was the late-night talks with his father, talks that had gradually transitioned from superficial to levels of sharing she'd never experienced with anyone else.

Whatever the reason, the barriers she'd kept up for years had gradually crumbled. Now she found herself head over heels in love with a man she'd never have, because his heart still belonged to someone else.

That kiss had proved it. At first, it was amazement, anticipation and joy all rolled into one heart-pounding, ground-shifting experience. Then everything changed. She knew the moment it shifted. The kiss was no longer hers. It was borrowed, maybe even stolen. Because it belonged to his deceased wife.

She slowed the rental car as she approached Colton's property. The insurance adjuster had notified her yesterday that they'd be totaling hers. Tomorrow she'd begin the search for a new one.

When she reached Colton's driveway, he'd already opened the gate for her. She killed the engine and stepped from the vehicle, pulse pounding with a mix of nervousness and excitement. She'd hadn't seen them since they'd returned to Murphy after Colton's twenty-four-hour hospital stay. But they'd had daily phone conversations and even Skyped a few times.

She made her way up the front walk to the deck. The living room curtains were open, framing the still-decorated Christmas tree. Maybe that was one of Colton's traditions—putting away Christmas on New Year's Day. They'd decorated together; maybe they'd undecorate together.

Moments after she rapped on the door, it swung open. Colton stood inside, weight shifted to his left leg, a crutch tucked under each arm.

He extended both arms. "Happy New Year."

If the strength of his embrace was any indication, he'd missed her as much as she'd missed him.

"Jasmine!"

She pulled away from Colton to find Liam running full speed toward her. He didn't stop until he'd slammed into her and wound both arms around her legs.

Laughing, she clutched the doorjamb for support, then disentangled herself so she could pick him up. "Have you been a good boy for your daddy?"

Liam nodded.

When her gaze met Colton's, his eyes held seriousness. "Your name is the first thing he's said since the kidnapping."

Her heart fluttered, partly from Colton's words and partly from the warmth in his gaze.

She put Liam down and bent to pet Brutus. His greeting was less exuberant than Liam's, but just as joyful. Since the moment she entered, he'd stood staring up at her, tail wagging.

Colton retrieved a small package from under the tree

and handed it to her. "Today is happy New Year and be-lated merry Christmas all in one. I forgot to give it to you before you left. I brought it to Atlanta with me on Christ-mas, but with everything that happened, I forgot again."

After putting Liam on the floor, she tore off the wrapping paper to reveal a small hinged box. It held a gold locket, Liam's picture inside. "I love it." She worked the fine chain free of the slots and held it up.

After Colton had fastened it around her neck, he extended an arm toward the kitchen. "Lunch is ready."

When she turned that way, she drew in a sharp breath. A white tablecloth covered the small table. A dozen red roses occupied a vase at one end, candles burning on both sides. The places were set with china, even Liam's.

"Wow, this is a bit fancy for just lunch, isn't it?"

"It's not 'just lunch.'"

Ignoring her raised brows, he removed a covered cas-serole from the oven and placed it on one of the three pot holders on the table.

She strapped Liam into his high chair. "What can I do to help?"

"You can pour our tea and put some milk into one of Liam's sippy cups."

When finished, she moved to the table, where three hot baking dishes waited. Colton removed their lids, and a variety of aromas wrapped around her. Her stomach rumbled. There was some kind of chicken dish, a potato casserole and green beans with sliced almonds.

After Colton slid serving spoons into each, he sat next to Liam. She took a seat opposite Colton. An envelope lay facedown on the table in front of the roses. She eyed it, curious about what was inside. With all he'd done to make a beautiful presentation, he wouldn't have left a piece of mail lying on the table. It was there for a reason.

Colton grasped his son's hand, then reached across the table to take hers. When he'd finished blessing the food, he indicated the serving spoon in the chicken. "Help yourself."

She dished up a large breast swimming in some kind of delectable sauce.

"Did you make all this?" Either his cooking skills had improved in the past few weeks or he'd gotten some help.

"Okay, I admit it. I enlisted some help from Paige. I was hoping to impress you. Have I succeeded?"

"If it tastes half as good as it smells, you have." After spooning the other two items onto her plate, she looked across the table at Colton. "I went to church yesterday."

A smile climbed up his cheeks. "Awesome."

"When those guys had Liam and we'd lost you, I prayed. And God answered. I figured it was time to look more seriously into this faith you have."

"And how was the service?"

"Good. I'll definitely be back."

The conversation over lunch was light. Colton hadn't gone back to work yet but hoped the doctor would release him in another week or two, even if he needed the help of crutches. By then Paige would have returned to school, so Liam would go back to day care.

Liam had had two nightmares since they'd come home several days ago. At least the frequency hadn't increased from what it had been before. Maybe the kidnapping didn't traumatize him as much as they'd feared. Apparently, the kidnappers had treated him well.

As they conversed, she shifted her gaze to the envelope several times, unable to shake the feeling that the light conversation was a prequel to something much weightier. Apparently, Colton planned to make her wait until the end of the meal to find out what.

After lunch, she cleared the dishes while Colton served up three pieces of cheesecake and poured a blueberry glaze over them. Ten minutes later, all the plates were empty.

Colton sat back and rubbed his stomach. "That hit the spot."

"That did more than hit the spot. I feel like I've just been served a gourmet meal."

"I have to give Paige all the credit."

"Not *all* the credit. I doubt she did all this on her own initiative."

The smile he gave her made her chest constrict. It figured. After a history of falling for guys who were bad news, she'd finally found one perfect for her and someone else had gotten him first.

Colton stood and returned moments later with a wet cloth. After cleaning the blueberry glaze from his son's fingers, he handed the envelope to Liam. "How about giving Miss Jasmine her card?"

A smile spread across Liam's face as he passed it to her.

She removed the card from the envelope and read the script. "May the year ahead be filled with unexpected blessings…"

When she opened it, a folded piece of paper fell to the table. Before picking it up, she read the words on the inside of the card. "…and joy beyond measure."

It was signed, "Love, Colton and Liam."

She looked at Liam, then his father. "Thank you."

When she picked up what had fallen to the table, Liam clapped his hands, excitement radiating from him. It was a piece of computer paper, folded in fourths. She opened it slowly.

Large crayon letters filled the page—

Will you please marry my daddy?

Her heart stuttered to a stop, then kick-started in a crazy rhythm. She longed to say yes. Colton was everything she wanted in a man. He was the answer to what she'd longed for even before she could put it into words. And even though she'd fought it with everything in her, she'd fallen hopelessly in love with him.

His grief over the loss of his wife drew her to him in a way she'd never expected. They'd both lost someone dear to them, and it had created a special bond.

But there was a difference. She'd moved past her loss. He hadn't.

She met Colton's gaze. "And how does his daddy feel?"

"His daddy wants this as much as Liam does."

She shook her head. Colton wanted it because he felt it was best for his son.

"I'm not Mandy. And I can't live under her shadow. From what I've gathered, she was everything I'm not. I can't compete. I won't even try."

"No, you're not Mandy."

She flinched at the words, even though she'd just said them herself. Even though they were true. She lowered her gaze to her hands, folded on the table over the card.

"You're Jasmine. And you're every bit as incredible."

She again met his eyes.

"You have qualities she didn't have, qualities that I admire just as much. Although you had no nurturing yourself, you have an innate sense of how to make Liam feel loved and secure. In spite of your upbringing, you've become an amazing woman. You're strong and brave. You'd throw yourself in front of a train if it meant protecting someone you cared about."

She shook her head. "You'll never have with me what

you had with your wife. Every relationship I've had has failed."

"Maybe you were looking for the wrong things with the wrong guys." He reached for the crutches he'd leaned against the wall.

As soon as he stood, Liam raised both arms. "Down?"

His attention shifted to his son, and she expelled a relieved sigh. She needed space, the opportunity to digest everything he'd just said.

She didn't have long. Within moments, Colton had wiped his son's hands and placed him on the floor. Two seconds later, Liam was running for his room.

Colton circled the table and pulled out the chair next to her. "I've been fighting feelings for you since the first time I saw you comforting my son. I believed if I gave in, I wouldn't be honoring Mandy's memory."

"What changed?"

"A stern talking-to by some meddling friends. When Tanner and Bryce came to see me in the hospital, they said things I didn't want to hear. But they got me thinking."

He took her hands in his. "Over the last few days, I've come to realize some things. First, Liam isn't going to remember his mother, no matter what I do to keep her memory alive. He's just too young."

He drew in a deep breath. "Second, in trying to honor my wife's memory, I've neglected what I know her wishes would be."

"And what's that?"

"To do what's best for both Liam and me. That's having you in our lives."

He squeezed her hands. "I love you, Jasmine. And I'm asking if you'll marry me. If you won't say yes to Liam's cute little note, will you say yes to my heartfelt proposal?"

Warmth surged through her as if a geyser had erupted inside. Behind her eyes, pressure built. And heat. Several seconds passed before she recognized the sensation for what it was.

No, she wasn't going to cry. She'd experienced hardship and sorrow. She'd seen death. Many times. She railed in anger. She punched things. She stormed off to be alone and gain control over her emotions.

But she didn't cry. Not ever.

That was exactly what was happening, though.

The heat built. Tears overflowed her lashes and trickled down her face.

"Jasmine? What did I say?"

"I'm sorry." At least she wasn't doing the ugly cry she'd seen on some women, eyes squeezed shut and face contorted. It was just these silent, stubborn tears making rivulets down her cheeks. "I'm not upset. I'm happy."

And that was the problem.

She handled adversity with amazing strength. But this wasn't adversity. It was joy. Maybe one reason she never cried was because she'd never been this deliriously happy.

She swiped at the tears streaming down her face. "How about if I say yes to both?"

As he pulled her to her feet, Liam returned to the kitchen holding his latest Lego creation. He raised it for their inspection.

Colton took it from him and looked at it from every angle. "This is a pretty amazing house. Did you do this all by yourself?"

Liam nodded, a big smile climbing up his cheeks, and Jasmine offered her own praise.

Courtship was going to be different with a little one. And when she and Colton entered marriage, it would be as a threesome. Not what she'd envisioned for her life.

But she wouldn't have it any other way.

She watched Colton hand him back the miniature house. "What are you going to have him call me?"

"Anything he wants."

"Even if it's *Mommy*?"

"Especially if it's *Mommy*."

Liam ran off to his room to play. After wrapping her in his arms, Colton pressed his lips to hers, then pulled back. Hesitation filled his eyes. "Are you sure you're ready for this?"

"I'm positive."

"You're giving up your freedom."

"It's a small price to pay for what I'm getting in return."

He searched her eyes. "And this is what you want?"

"I want you. And I want Liam." She heaved a sigh. "Shut up and kiss me."

All his hesitation dissolved. He pulled her closer. When he slanted his mouth across hers, her knees went weak.

There was nothing borrowed about this kiss. It was hers and hers alone.

Colton was hers.

And he always would be.

One hundred percent.

EPILOGUE

Colton walked down the sidewalk with Jasmine's hand in his. The Valley River flowed lazily by on his left. On his right, a soft blanket of lawn stretched upward. A brief shower had passed through while they'd been in church, and the landscape now shone with a post-rain brilliance.

Behind them, Bryce and Andi carried on a conversation. Paige and Tanner brought up the rear. Four children danced down the path ahead of them, one several heads taller than the other three. They'd all finished a picnic at Konehete Park. Now the kids were having trouble containing their excitement over a promised playground visit.

"Slow down." Colton used his authoritative parent voice. "You're getting too far ahead of us."

Liam cast a quick glance over his shoulder before turning back around to corral his younger playmates. As Colton watched his son give directions, then shift from instructor to buddy, he couldn't stop his smile. If he hadn't lived those agonizing months himself, he'd never believe the joyful, energetic boy in front of him had ever been the sad, silent child who'd occupied his home three and a half years ago.

And during those dark weeks after Mandy's death, he would never have anticipated that in a few short years Liam would have a perky, dark-haired little sister.

Just past the tennis courts, the kids made a sharp right to follow the path that led away from the river. They knew the way to the playground. They'd been there often enough. Picnics in the park, followed by playtime, were a regular occurrence for all of them.

Andi and Bryce had been the first to announce their good news. Three months later, Paige had learned she was expecting. Three months after that, Jasmine had awoken nauseated.

For a full trimester, all three women were in one stage or another of expanding bellies and raging hormones. Tanner had insisted it was something in the water. Colton had sat back in wonder, amazed at the unexpected blessings God had brought into his life.

When they reached the fenced playground, Colton's little girl slid her hand into his and pointed.

Liam stepped up next to her. "Lacey wants you to push her on the swings."

Although she was two years old, Colton's daughter spoke very little. It wasn't that she didn't know how. With a protective big brother who anticipated her every desire, she probably didn't feel the need.

Paige grinned. "Swing time with Daddy sounds like a great idea." She turned toward Tanner and waved her hands in a shooing motion. "The ladies have more scheming to do."

Colton laughed. It was that time again. The three couples had done combined family vacations for the past three years. From what he'd overheard, this year's plans involved renting a motorhome.

He led his two friends toward the swings, then lifted Lacey into one. Soon Tanner's son swung on one side of her, Bryce's on the other. Being the only girl in their foursome had never seemed to bother Lacey.

When Colton sought out the women, they were seated on one of the park benches, huddled over their cell phones. Paige said something and passed hers to Andi, who then showed it to Jasmine. Probably an interesting travel destination.

Paige had completed her degree and gotten her teaching certification. Next week, she would finish her first year as a fifth-grade teacher. Andi was still managing her party store and doing special events decorating.

Of the three women, it was Jasmine's path that had taken the greatest deviation. After she and Colton had gotten married, she'd given up her job with Burch Security and gone to work part-time for the Cherokee County Sheriff's Office. Nine months later, Lacey showed up. Jasmine took temporary leave and never went back. She'd said she would. Someday.

Colton hadn't pushed. She stayed plenty busy chasing around two active children, besides volunteering at MountainView and assisting Andi with the occasional decorating job. During the time she'd been a full-time mom, Liam had flourished. Lacey also seemed to enjoy having her around.

When Colton looked at Bryce, he, too, was watching the three women.

Bryce spoke without looking at him. "What do you think they're planning?"

"A cross-country trip. Or maybe Canada. Just a guess."

Tanner nodded. "I wouldn't mind seeing Canada again."

"Yeah." Colton knew where his friend's mind had gone. The same place his own had—the two-week rafting and backpacking trip the three of them had taken years ago. That had been when they were young, single guys, without the responsibilities of wives and children.

Bryce sighed. "Remember when vacations meant hang gliding, rock climbing or finding some other way to pit ourselves against the forces of nature?"

Tanner's response held a touch of nostalgia. "Yeah."

"You guys ever miss it?"

Colton didn't have to think about his answer for long. "Miss it? Sometimes. Regret where I am now? Not a chance."

He was married to an amazing woman. He had a happy, well-adjusted son. Both were blessings he'd never expected to receive. As if that wasn't enough, his world was enriched even further by a beautiful little girl.

Regrets? Not a one.

He wouldn't trade the life he had now for all the wealth in the world.

* * * * *

*If you enjoyed this exciting story of
suspense and intrigue,
pick up these other stories from Carol J. Post:*

Shattered Haven
Hidden Identity
Mistletoe Justice
Buried Memories
Reunited by Danger
Fatal Recall
Lethal Legacy

Available now from Love Inspired Suspense!

Find more great reads at www.LoveInspired.com

Dear Reader,

I hope you've enjoyed our final visit with our Murphy friends. At the suggestion of both my editor and my critique partner, I decided to change it up and have the heroine protecting the hero rather than the other way around.

Colton's life was shattered with the sudden loss of his wife, then was turned upside down again when someone threatened his son. When circumstances brought Jasmine into his life, though, he found that sometimes God allows healing to come from unexpected sources.

Jasmine had a difficult time accepting the idea of a personal God who would allow bad things to happen to those who serve Him. But sometimes God delivers His people from the storms, and other times He walks us through them. In both situations, when we look for it, we can see the hand of a loving Heavenly Father.

I pray God's blessings on your life and peace through whatever storms you face.

Love in Christ,
Carol J. Post

SPECIAL EXCERPT FROM

Love Inspired
SUSPENSE

*With a price on his witness's head,
US marshal Jonathan Mast can think of only
one place to hide Celeste Alexander—in the
Amish community he left behind. But will this trip
home save their lives…and convince them that a
Plain life together is worth fighting for?*

Read on for a sneak preview of
Amish Hideout *by Maggie K. Black,
the exciting beginning to the Amish Witness Protection
miniseries, available January 2019
from Love Inspired Suspense!*

Time was running out for Celeste Alexander. Her fingers
flew over the keyboard, knowing each keystroke could be
her last before US marshal Jonathan Mast arrived to escort
her to her new life in the witness protection program.

"You gave her a laptop?" US marshal Stacy Preston
demanded. "Please tell me you didn't let her go online."

"Of course not! She had a basic tablet, with the internet
capability disabled." US marshal Karl Adams shot back
even before Stacy had finished her sentence.

The battery died. She groaned. Well, that was that.

"You guys mind if I go upstairs and get my charging
cable?"

LISEXP1218

The room went black. Then she heard the distant sound of gunfire erupting outside.

"Get Celeste away from the windows!" Karl shouted. "I'll cover the front."

What was happening? She felt Stacy's strong hand on her arm pulling her out of her chair.

"Come on!" Stacy shouted. "We have to hurry—"

Her voice was swallowed up in the sound of an explosion, expanding and roaring around them, shattering the windows, tossing Celeste backward and engulfing the living room in smoke. Celeste hit the floor, rolled and hit a door frame. She crawled through it, trying to get away from the smoke billowing behind her.

Suddenly a strong hand grabbed her out of the darkness, taking her by the arm and pulling her up to her feet so sharply she stumbled backward into a small room. The door closed behind them. She opened her mouth to scream, but a second hand clamped over her mouth. A flashlight flickered on and she looked up through the smoky haze, past worn blue jeans and a leather jacket, to see the strong lines of a firm jaw trimmed with a black beard, a straight nose and serious eyes staring into hers.

"Celeste Alexander?" He flashed a badge. "I'm Marshal Jonathan Mast. Stay close. I'll keep you safe."

Don't miss
Amish Hideout *by Maggie K. Black,*
available January 2019 wherever
Love Inspired® Suspense books and ebooks are sold.

www.LoveInspired.com

Looking for inspiration in tales
of hope, faith and heartfelt romance?

Check out **Love Inspired**® and
Love Inspired® **Suspense** books!

New books available every month!

CONNECT WITH US AT:

Facebook.com/groups/HarlequinConnection

Facebook.com/HarlequinBooks

Twitter.com/HarlequinBooks

Instagram.com/HarlequinBooks

Pinterest.com/HarlequinBooks

ReaderService.com

Love Inspired®